**Spring wished she had
artistic talent. She'd love to capture
Chad on paper as he looked
this very moment.**

His hair reflected golden streaks under the
lamplight, and the shadowed light gave his
nose strength while it softened the tired lines
around his mouth. An unexpected tenderness
crept over her; she wanted so badly to smooth
those lines away, to feel the texture of his skin
beneath her fingers.

The man needed to go to bed...to sleep solidly
until morning. It couldn't hurt to merely
suggest he call it a night.

She lowered herself beside him, keeping her
focus squarely on his face. She leaned forward
to place her hand on his shoulder. His soft
breath brushed her skin, sending a quiver up
her arm.

Books by Ruth Scofield

Love Inspired

In God's Own Time #29
The Perfect Groom #65
Whispers of the Heart #89
Wonders of the Heart #124

RUTH SCOFIELD

became serious about writing after she'd raised her children. Until then, she'd concentrated her life on being a June Cleaver-type wife and mother, spent years as a Bible student and teacher for teens and young adults and led a weekly women's prayer group. When she'd made a final wedding dress and her last child had left the nest, she declared to one and all that it was her turn to activate a dream. Thankfully, her husband applauded her decision.

Ruth began school in an old-fashioned rural two-room schoolhouse and grew up in the days before television, giving substance to her notion that she still has one foot in the last century. However, active involvement with six rambunctious grandchildren has her eagerly looking forward to the next millennium. After living on the East Coast for years, Ruth and her husband now live in Missouri.

Wonders of the Heart
Ruth Scofield

Published by Steeple Hill Books™

STEEPLE HILL BOOKS

ISBN 0-373-87131-7

WONDERS OF THE HEART

Copyright © 2001 by Ruth Scofield Schmidt

Visit us at www.steeplehill.com

Printed in U.S.A.

But seek first His kingdom and His righteousness, and all these things will be given to you as well.
—*Matthew* 6:33

Now faith is being sure of what we hope for and certain of what we do not see. This is what the ancients were commended for.
—*Hebrews* 11:1-2

To the BICC gang.
May you all continue long and creatively
as each of you balance life with gracious dedication
to love, family, your talent and our Father.
And to my daughters, Karen, Laura and Lisa,
who do the same. God bless you.

Chapter One

Chad Alexander unlocked the door and entered his apartment. Too tired and hungry for comfort, he wondered if there was anything edible left in his kitchen. He should've swallowed his distaste for airport food, he guessed now, and grabbed something before starting for home. He didn't think he had any energy left to visit Harry's Grill, the closest place where he could order a decent meal.

He listened for his sister, Honor Suzanne.

On first observation, the apartment was fairly quiet. A CD played. He recognized the music only as a classical piece. One table lamp shed a narrow stream of light from the living room.

He set his bags down in the foyer, habit making him glance at the hall table for any mail that had caught up to him. Picking up the half-dozen on top, he stepped from the hall into the living room.

A blur of dark diaphanous skirts flashed by him in a whirl, bringing him up short. A pale bare foot paused, burrowing deep into the smooth off-white carpet, while its mate rose eye-high, arched and pointy-toed. Shapely arms reached high, fingers poised in a graceful arch. Ever slowly, the head bent backward on a delicate neck. Dark locks swung free of the dancer's shoulders creating a graceful motion into the air.

Caught up in the beauty of the dancer, he could only stare for a long moment. This wasn't his sister.

Spotting him, the young woman returned his look from upside down and froze. "Oh! Oh, my!" She righted herself instantly and spun to glare at him. "Who are you?"

A moment before, he'd thought her to be a friend of his sister's, but now he revised his opinion. She was older than fourteen-year-old Honor Suzanne by a good five years.

"I may well ask you the same," he said with sudden suspicion. What was this young woman doing here? Was she a neighbor? A dance teacher? He hadn't authorized the expenditure, though he had no objection.

"I live here," she answered, her blue-green eyes taking on a suspicious glint of their own.

He saw her gaze run over his unshaven jaw and wrinkled sport coat, giving him the impression she evaluated him with a decisive checklist in mind.

"How did you get in? I can call Security, you know."

"That isn't necessary," he muttered, letting irony lace his words. If he'd been a burglar or otherwise bad guy, her actions held all the intimidation of a mouse's. "I have a key."

"You do?"

"I do. Where's Mrs. Hinkle?"

"Who?"

He hardened his jaw, as her gaze went a little wider. Did she think he'd buy that innocent act? What was she trying to pull? Some kind of scam? Something was definitely out of kilter here. "Mrs. Hinkle. Where is she?"

"Um." She pursed her nicely shaped lips into a pretty pout. "Sir, are you sure you have the right apartment? Perhaps—"

Just a shade too polite. Not a New Yorker. She was a good actress, he'd give her that.

Was that it? Was she one of the many young things who came to New York every year hoping to break into theater, and she'd conned her way into his household?

"Uh-uh. You can't pull that." His irritation boiled to the surface and he stepped closer, eyes narrowed. "This is *my* apartment."

"I think, sir—" She retreated, two spots of color blossoming in her cheeks. Her gaze never wavered from his face as she fumbled behind her for the phone lying on the shadowed lamp table. "—that you should identify yourself immediately, or I will call Security.''

''That's an excellent idea, missy. Call Security. And you may identify *your*self! And tell me where my sister is,'' he demanded, his tone harsh and threatening. ''Explain what you've done with her.''

''Chad!'' Honor Suzanne shouted behind him. She quickly stepped around and into the room to stand beside the young woman. ''Here I am—don't get yourself into a twist. Nothing's wrong.''

''Honor,'' he croaked. He waited a moment to let his pounding heart slow down. ''It's about time you made an appearance. I thought— I was beginning to think the worst.''

''Well, there isn't a worst. At least, not now,'' Honor insisted. ''This is Spring. And you don't have to scare us out of our back teeth. It's late and you're home early. We didn't expect you till next week.''

''Sorry,'' he mumbled, glancing at his watch. Ten o'clock wasn't late by New York standards. Unclenching his hands, he twitched a shoulder in irritation. Why should he apologize for coming home at any time he chose?

Spring continued to stare at him, eyes wide, then she abruptly caught her breath as though breaking a spell.

''Chad.'' Her color spread into her hairline. ''Of course. I should've known. I'm so sorry. I'm the one to apologize, and I do so humbly. You obviously didn't remember about me being here. I'm Spring Barbour."

She thrust her hand forward in a rather formal offer to shake hands. He took it slowly, enveloping her slender fingers and palm in his for a required moment. He felt the delicate bones beneath, and slid a thumb across warm skin.

"I don't recall being told of your presence at all," he murmured.

"Oh, really?" she said with a slight frown in Honor Suzanne's direction. "Sorry. I suppose that information must have been lost along the way? But you don't look like those snapshots Honor has of you, do you? Not much, anyway. My goodness, they must've been taken ages ago. Otherwise, I would've recognized you right off. You should have something professionally done, really."

She dropped his hand, leaving his palm with a sense of loss. "But it doesn't matter now..." She trailed off.

Good. She'd hushed. He'd begun to think she never breathed. Yet her voice was soft, with a gentle accent.

He glanced at his sister, wondering about her choice in friends. At twenty years her senior, he didn't know much about teenagers, and supposed he'd have to study a bit to get up to speed.

Spring moved to turn off the CD player, her midnight blue skirts, made of some floaty material, dancing around her ankles. Raveling threads tickled her toes. He noticed for the first time that the hem wasn't stitched. He'd already noted she had only one sleeve in the top, the neckline slanting to reveal a graceful white throat. Her dark hair fell like feathers against her bare shoulders.

"That's a long ride in from the airport, isn't it?" she picked up again as she turned back. "What time did you land?"

"Couple of hours ago," he muttered, wondering who and what she was. He still wanted to know where Mrs. Hinkle had gone, thinking the woman had better have a doggone excellent excuse for allowing this young person to move into his apartment.

Where was the girl sleeping? He'd had to give up his den to accommodate the housekeeper. Another body in his apartment would put a big crunch in his life, on his space. And privacy. He had enough adjustments to face as it was.

"I'll just bet you're hungry," Spring continued. "Did you have anything? No? Honor, did you finish that English paper?"

"Uh-huh. Eight pages," Honor said, looking pleased. "It's much better now, since you showed me where I missed my theme. Bound to pull an *A*."

"Good. Then you can start the tea kettle while I change. I'll only be a minute. Chad, why don't you go on into the kitchen with Honor, and I'll be there in a minute to find something for you to eat."

"*You* will?" Why should she? He could take care of himself. And he wasn't a guest!

And where was that blasted housekeeper?

But his words only trailed her, as Spring disappeared down the hall. He turned to his sister. "Where's Mrs. Hinkle?"

"Um, Chad..." Honor laid a hand on his arm, anxiously coaxing him past the dining room alcove and into the kitchen. "Mrs. Hinkle isn't here."

"I can see that." The dining alcove was a mess. The table was covered with some of the same dark cloth Spring wore, and a sewing machine sat at the end. Scraps and loose threads lay on the floor. He yanked his gaze back to his sister's face. "Where is she?"

"I fired her."

"Excuse me?" He halted in the middle of the small kitchen, realizing that something had changed there, but unable to give it the attention it deserved in the face of Honor Suzanne's news. "You can't be serious."

"Well, I am. I did. I hired Spring, instead."

"You *what?*" He couldn't believe what he'd heard. No one in their right mind would allow a fourteen-year-old to hire or fire an employee. What had the employment agency said? Who had she talked with?

"I hired Spring..."

"How could you? What about the employment agency?"

"They didn't have much to say about it after the letter I wrote. I didn't like Mrs. Hinkle."

"Now wait a minute. You wrote a letter to the agency? Why, what was the need?"

"I told you, I didn't like Mrs. Hinkle."

"You said nothing before I left about not liking Mrs. Hinkle. Why didn't you inform me? Talk to me? And merely not liking her isn't enough reason to take such drastic action."

"I tried to talk to you once, but…" Honor turned away to fill an enameled tea kettle he'd never seen with bottled water, before setting it on a burner. "Well, you were so busy, and, anyway, I didn't know about Mrs. Hinkle until after you left."

The mild statement, carrying a good degree of guilt, hit him straight between the eyes. He hadn't heard Honor because he'd been too busy to listen to her teenage twaddle.

He hid his sense of frustration, and mentally chided himself. He might not have been eager to take Honor Suzanne into his life, but he'd had no other choice when she'd become so depressed after their father died, only two years after Honor's mother had passed away. Now he was all she had, her only living relative.

He ran a hand against his jaw and turned away to shed his jacket. True, he'd been too involved in getting his last-minute arrangements in place for an extended absence to interview many candidates. It all had happened at once; Honor coming to live with him as he was preparing for a working trip through several European countries.

"Tell me why you didn't like Mrs. Hinkle," he said, pulling out one of two kitchen chairs at the tiny table meant for one. "She came well recommended by the agency. Couldn't you have lived with your dislike until I got home?"

"No, I couldn't. She was impossible. And I don't know why they recommended her," she muttered. "She steals."

"Steals?" He frowned, silently questioning how such a woman could have gotten past the agency screening. "Are you sure? Could you have misinterpreted something you saw?"

"No, I didn't, Chad."

She thrust out her small chin, reminding him of her mother, Sandra. He hadn't liked Sandra.

"I saw her going through your desk," Honor insisted.

"I left my desk double-locked." Uneasiness began to set in. He didn't keep a lot of important papers in his home office unless he was working there, but he still didn't like the idea of anything being disturbed. He did keep a list of his private bank numbers and associated interactions in a notebook in the bottom drawer, but it would have to be an experienced thief to take advantage of the coded knowledge.

He'd check his desk contents before going to bed, but said now, "Well, there isn't anything of movable cash value in there, anyway. And I left the household funds in a special account. Mrs. Hinkle only had to charge anything else you needed.''

''Well, she pried the desk open,'' Honor insisted. She reached for a pig-faced cookie jar, half-filled, which he'd never seen. ''In fact, you can see scratches on the brass key holes, if you look closely.''

Frowning, he rubbed the base of his neck where a headache was forming. The problem was more serious than he'd thought. ''What did you do? Why didn't you call me?''

''I didn't think I should bother you with it, Chad. You said you wouldn't have time to keep track of what's going on at home. Uncle Walter and Mr. Lester took care of it.''

Walter Peebles, his father's friend and accountant, and Lester Brown, their building super. He'd have a long talk with Lester first thing in the morning. Right before he called the agency.

He'd reach Walter before he went to bed.

''Didn't want to be bothered?'' Guilt nearly choked him now; he *had* said it. He'd failed royally as a brother. ''Honor, I merely meant I wouldn't have time for, um—uh-oh, stuff it. I'd have *taken* time to deal with this problem, whatever it was.''

He took a cookie from the plate Honor set on the table. Home-baked oatmeal, a longtime favorite.

''But you said you were really, really busy on this trip and for me not to expect a lot of communication

from you since you'd be moving around a lot,"
Honor persisted, half-accusing.

She poured boiling water into an old, crackled ce-
ramic teapot and covered it with a bright red cover.
The teapot was another item he didn't remember.

"You couldn't come home till your business was
finished, that's what you said."

She set out three china cups; at last, something he
recognized. Vaguely. He couldn't remember the last
time he'd entertained at home, but he thought those
to be the ones his girlfriend of two years ago had
purchased for him.

Honor set out a small jar of honey, and spoons.
"So I decided to handle it myself. And I had Dana's
help."

"Who's Dana?"

"Dana Bates. My minister's wife. She knows
about these things, Chad, and she helped me find
Spring."

"Hmmm… A minister and his wife." He rubbed
his jaw, then ran his hand against the back of his
head, while visions of smug, do-gooding people
marched through his thoughts. That's all he
needed—interference from another direction. He'd
had enough of that from well-meaning old family
friends after his father died, leaving his estate in a
mess.

He probably should put this off until he'd had
some sleep; after all, Honor was safe and sound, and

he couldn't pursue an investigation on anything stolen until morning. But...he wouldn't.

"All right." He let his breath out on a long-suffering note. "Tell me about Spring. Last name. Who is she? Where is she from? Where did you find her? What are her references? And *how old* is she?"

Chapter Two

"My name is Spring Eve Barbour, and I do assure you, Mr. Alexander, I'm a very reputable person."

Spring stood in the kitchen doorway, addressing Chad formally, letting him in on her awareness of the seriousness of his questions. She didn't feel at all nervous, trusting in Uncle William's dictates to always deal with the truth, but she thought if she'd had anything to hide, Chad's narrowed stare might unnerve her.

"I'll be glad to trot out my references if you want to see them, but Dana will verify that she checked my credibility and found that I am who I am and all that stuff before Honor and I struck our bargain."

Spring moved into the small kitchen on this last. She took into account the deep lines fanning Chad's eyes and the taut skin across his cheekbones, and

wondered if he'd stay awake long enough to eat anything even if she prepared it.

Opening the refrigerator door, she stared at the
contents to determine what might be the quickest
thing to serve. He'd want something hot, she
thought, but a man that seriously tired also needed
something reasonably balanced on his stomach before he went to bed.

"How about scrambled eggs and ham?" She
turned to look at him over her shoulder as she asked.
He'd removed his jacket and tie, and unbuttoned his
shirt a few buttons down. His head rested against the
wall, causing his eyes to go half-mast, the blue irises
deepening to a dark stirring.

They caused a stirring in her middle, too. Something that spread throughout her like hot sweet cider
in her mouth, with a spicy kick on the edges of her
tongue.

"And, um, I'm twenty-three." Why that was suddenly important, she didn't know—except that she
wanted him to know. She might be new to the Big
Apple, but she wasn't too young and naive to care
for a young girl.

Yet that wasn't the only reason she wanted him
to know she was well past legal...for anything.

"Twenty-three," he repeated as though he didn't
quite believe her. His quick glance down her faded
jeans and T-shirt didn't help her cause.

Spring knew she didn't look her age. Her twin,
Autumn, and she had found it rather funny these last

few years when someone mistook them for younger, but it had never been a real problem. A little makeup usually helped, but she seldom wore it unless she was going out.

Since he hadn't said no to the eggs, she pulled out the egg carton and other ingredients, and faced the counter and stove top to work, which gave him her back to view.

Spring no longer wondered about his skepticism. It was natural. While she'd heard all about Honor's problems with her predecessor, obviously Chad had gone about his business in ignorance. She hadn't given much thought to the fact that his messages from Europe were sketchy. She'd thought Chad had been informed about the change in the household. About her being there.

Now she was in an awkward position.

"Honor, why don't you toast a couple of biscuits, too. Or—" she glanced at Chad again, gauging his reaction "—would you prefer toast? All we have on hand is wheat bread."

"Whatever you have is fine," he muttered. "And yes, I think I would like to see those references, if you don't mind."

"All right. I'll find them while you eat."

"Really, Chad, you don't have to do that," Honor protested. "Dana already checked all of Spring's references and found them excellent. Besides, Spring really helped me out of a jam, and we get along terrifically. You just don't know—"

"That's just it, kiddo. I *don't* know. And I do need to see them. What kind of a lawyer would I be if I didn't pay close attention to details? Or follow up? It's my job to look into the inner workings of corporate issues and mergers, and make sure the reported backgrounds and company assets and potential is as stated."

"But I couldn't have—"

"He's quite right, Honor," Spring said, sending her young friend a "Cool it" glance. She'd corner Honor later over this lack of communication, but now wasn't the time. "He'd be a poor kind of brother to accept me at face value without checking my references, when we live together. Um, rather, when I live in your apartment and come from who-knows-where, as far as he knows."

Her agreement didn't seem to placate him much, but Chad's attention turned to the plate of fluffy eggs and slice of warmed ham she set before him.

A moment later, Honor retrieved a couple of biscuits from the toaster oven, split, buttered, then browned under the broiler as Spring had shown her. She placed them next to his plate.

Spring found the sugarless strawberry jam and set it in the center of the table.

Spring stepped back and folded her hands in front of her. On the other side of Chad, Honor shifted from one foot to the other, pursing her mouth. Chad looked from his sister to her, then down at his plate.

It struck Spring that they were like two young

servant girls from a century ago, hovering over the master to see what else they could do to please him. She wanted to laugh at her mental image, drawn from reading all those English classics of which Uncle William approved. Plus the historical novels she read undercover, to which she'd been addicted in her teen years.

She bit her lip to keep her giggle under control. Honor gave her a puzzled glance, to which she answered with a slight shake of her head.

Spring did miss her sister. Autumn would have read her mind instantly, and understood her line of thought. Even if Spring explained it, Honor Suzanne was simply too young to catch the humor.

Then she saw the rising suspicion in Chad's glinting dark blue eyes, and her humor vanished. He'd never get the joke.

Well, smothering him with kindness wasn't such a good idea, Spring decided. He wouldn't understand the attention as mere kindness, or he'd misinterpret it altogether.

Turning, she left the kitchen to search for her references. A month ago, she'd no notion that she'd find being a companion to a young girl to hold so much complication. Or fun, either. She and Honor got along as though born to be friends. Honor was as new to the city as she, and they'd been exploring Manhattan together in their free time.

A few moments later, she reentered the kitchen. Chad had nearly cleaned his plate, she quickly noted.

"...and you should see some of the collections! Funny stuff from a long time ago. Centuries, even," Honor said, telling of their recent visit to the Design Museum.

"Most of it wasn't funny when it was designed," Spring reminded her with a grin. "And a generation or two past doesn't quite make it into the 'centuries' category for Mrs. Pine or Mr. Steward, now does it?"

Chad raised a brow. "Who?"

"These old people at church," Honor explained, then hastily added, "But they're really neat. They, like, visited our Sunday night Jumpstart a couple of weeks ago and told us about how it was when they were teenagers. Mr. Steward enlisted in the Army to fight in World War II when he was only seventeen."

"What's Jumpstart?" Again, Chad raised a brow, but then lowered it into a frown. Finished eating, he leaned back in his chair and sipped his tea. Giving it a quick glance, Spring noticed his startled reaction at the herbal concoction. Yet he made no comment, merely returning his cup to its saucer.

"It's our weekly meeting for high schoolers, mostly," Honor explained. "Lots of college kids come, too. Only, we have more than just kids who attend. It's awesome, Chad. You should come sometime. Spring does, and—"

"What do you do there?"

"We Jumpstart the week with Bible Study and prayer and encouraging stuff. And Josh Nolan, our youth minister, usually talks, but it's not like a heavy sermon or anything.''

Chad's eyes began to droop.

''Perhaps you'd rather hear all of this tomorrow,'' Spring murmured, thinking they were losing his attention fast. It wasn't fair to overload an already exhausted mind, and expect that mind to later retain an ounce of intelligent memory, Uncle William used to say. Of course, he would say that especially when she and Autumn wanted to talk to him at the same time.

Spring smiled inwardly at the memory. Uncle William had died a few months before, having urged her and Autumn to pursue their dreams, and leaving each of them with a small legacy to do so.

Now she was having adventures in New York City.

Chad assessed her face a moment before saying, ''Some of it can wait. Right now, I want to know more about you, if you don't mind.''

''Sure. Of course. Here you go—'' She placed a copy of her resume in front of him. It gave her educational background and work and personal references from Kansas City, her hometown. She hadn't a wide range of worldly experience, she was ready to admit, but she felt perfectly confident in watching over Honor Suzanne and guiding her schoolwork. After all, she'd been the more nurturing of the two sisters at home, and could run a household with perfect ease.

"I attended a Midwest community college, which I know isn't very impressive by any of the big-school standards, but I've worked steadily since I turned eighteen and I have a good work ethic. Uncle William saw to that. He raised my sister Autumn, and me."

"What are you doing here in New York?" Chad asked.

"I'm a dress designer. Or I want to be. I've been putting in my applications around the city and showing some of my sketches."

"I see. And do your duties here leave you enough time for all that?" His tone had an edge of sarcasm, but Spring ignored it while Honor gazed adoringly at her brother.

"She's bound to be accepted someplace, Chad," Honor put in enthusiastically. "She's really good. That dress she was wearing when you came in is for one of the women in our church. She's a ballet dancer and needed a dressmaker, so Dana suggested—"

"You run a business out of this apartment?" Chad sat forward abruptly, his tone sharp.

"Well, it's not exactly a real business," Spring answered. "Only a little sewing."

"Do you accept money for your services?"

"Um, yes. A few dollars. But—"

"You must stop it immediately! This apartment is strictly residential and has an airtight code against

using it for business purposes. You could get us
fined or kicked out of our lease for such an offence.''

"Oh, I—I'm sorry. I didn't realize—''

"We didn't know that, Chad,'' Honor said, her
lower lip beginning to tremble. "Don't be mad. We
just thought to earn a little extra spending money…''

"Spending money? I think for what I pay you,''
he all but sputtered at Spring before turning to
Honor, "and your allowance, that you'd have quite
enough for mere pocket money. What have you been
buying, anyway?''

Spring decided it wasn't the time to inform him
she hadn't been paid, or that Honor hadn't received
an allowance for weeks. Already, she knew it would
disturb him. He'd learn the necessary details in due
time.

"Nothing out of reason, Mr. Alexander. Only
tickets to special exhibits and a few restaurant
meals.'' *Few* was the operative word, Spring
thought, with New York prices so much higher than
what she was used to. "But that didn't come out of
anyone's salary.''

"No, I'm sure it didn't. Household accounts, I
suppose. Well, I'll look at the receipts and do the
accounting tomorrow. You did keep receipts, didn't
you?''

Spring hadn't meant the expenditures had come
from the household accounts, but she guessed he'd
discover that soon enough, too. "Actually, I didn't
see a need.''

His frown deepened. "Really? How did you expect to justify the budget I left for you? What about the credit card bills?"

"I didn't see a budget." She brushed her bangs from her eyes, beginning to feel a little ruffled. "Sorry. But you'll find everything is in order since I've been here, and we have no outstanding bills. We simply pay cash as we go."

"Is there anything left from the discretionary fund I left for Mrs. Hinkle's use?"

"What discretionary fund?" Spring asked.

"No, Chad. That's what I wanted to tell you," Honor said. "There's nothing left in the cash account or the credit card limit. Mrs. Hinkle spent it all, including my allowance, in the first ten days after you left."

"What?" His mouth dropped as he tried to take in what Honor had said. "But there was enough there to cover everything except the most dire of emergencies, and she was directed to apply to Walter Peebles if there was any greater need. How could she have run through what should've lasted three months?"

"Well, she did. And Uncle Walter turned down a couple of requests she made to him. When I called Uncle Walter, he told me what to do. We notified all our credit card accounts, and closed out the two bank accounts and opened new ones. Dana and Spring helped me do that. But you have to sign the new bank cards, Uncle Walter said."

Chad brushed a hand over his face. Had he fallen through a rabbit hole?

"Let me get this right. You say Mrs. Hinkle took all the cash I'd left for spending money, cashed out the household account, and made inroads on the credit cards, and you caught her jimmying my desk, as well?"

"That's what I've been trying to tell you. Spring—"

"Good grief, Honor Suzanne—" Chad nearly shot out of his chair. "Why didn't you call me? What on earth were you thinking, not to inform me of such a huge problem?"

"Well, we did tell Uncle Walter. And we told him everything we'd done to take care of it, and he said we'd done the right things and he didn't see that anything more could be done until you got back and not to disturb you."

"Did he lend you money to get by on? Who's been paying the bills? What have you been using this last month for incidentals and such?"

"Oh, Chad, that's where you'll be so proud of me." Honor's adoring smile spread a charm all its own, Spring thought, a loveliness already showing the promise of womanhood.

"See, Spring and I reached a bargain. She lives here in exchange for being my adult companion and friend. No money exchanged. We share actual expenses. Isn't that a wow deal? Daddy would say my Alexander blood is showing up."

Chad remained quiet for a long moment, his gaze slowly returning to Spring's. "No money exchanged? Okay, then. What have you been living on for a month?"

"Well, our cupboards have become a little bare," Spring confessed with a quick smile. In truth, they had a need to do a major restocking. "But we have another sitting job lined up for tomorrow night."

"You've been living on baby-sitting pay?" he asked incredulously.

"Not totally," Spring replied.

"Then what have you been living on?"

"Well, I've paid into our mutual kitty a bit," she admitted.

His suspicious gaze went as icy as an Alaskan glacier. "All right. What do I owe you? I'm sure there's a payback for you. What is it you want?"

Spring sighed. Could this man be any more exasperating?

Chapter Three

"**Y**ou don't owe me anything, Mr. Alexander." Spring gave him a straight-on serious look to let him know she hadn't tried to take advantage of anyone, neither Honor nor him, in his recent absence. Though, she could understand his concern; she was yet a stranger. She certainly realized how difficult it had become these days to accept someone at simple face value.

"Honor and I made a fair exchange in our bargain," she continued, hoping he'd see the advantage to their arrangement right away. "And Mr. Peebles made sure all the necessary bills were paid, the utilities and things like that. Honor and I are bubbling along very well on our own. We merely earn extra spending money when we can."

"And how have you done that?"

His tone was so frosty, Spring thought he'd ice

up the remaining tea in her cup. That reminded her to pour him another of the still hot brew, but she only got a downward twist of his mouth for her trouble.

Oddly, she liked the way his mouth moved. Wide and sensual, she thought it very expressive. Right now Chad wasn't in a good mood. Understandably, he was tired and confused, and angry over matters that were beyond his control. But on a normal day, with a regular routine, when he felt comfortable and relaxed, his face would lighten a lot, wouldn't it? What would bring a smile to his mouth then? And what would that smile be like?

"Baby-sitting," Honor answered with pride. "But never alone and only in our apartment complex or for church families. And once, a mother paid us to run her little girl's birthday party. That was fun. We often get dinner, too, when we sit in the evenings, so we—"

"You *what!*"

His outrage stung. Honor fell silent, while Spring reassessed his temper. Maybe she'd underestimated his mood just a tad. She pushed the jam jar forward a bit, thinking he could use a little sweetening, and pointed out, "It's an honored profession, Mr. Alexander."

"Well, it may be," he said, pulling his mouth into a straight line. "But I don't want Honor to do it anymore. She doesn't have to work, and she's too young, just a kid. Whatever possessed you? I don't want her out on the streets, or out…out at night.''

"That's right, Chad, I'm a kid and kids baby-sit to earn money all the time.'' Honor's chin came out while her eyes flashed stubbornness. "There's nothing wrong in baby-sitting or having a job.''

"But to depend on getting dinner when you sit?''

"It's an accepted practice, Mr. Alexander,'' Spring added in a placating tone. "Even teens from wealthy families baby-sit, and often have supper with the children. And there's safety in being a team. I promise you, it isn't robbing Honor of study time, and we make a strict rule of being home by ten on a school night.''

"That's not the only thing that concerns me,'' he muttered. "If my associates get wind of this, they could misconstrue the entire situation.''

"Well, we needed the money,'' Honor said with a finalizing note. "And Daddy would have said I'm not too young to learn about balancing my finances.''

"Baby-sitting money?'' Chad shook his head. "How could you need that piddling amount? Surely, the matter isn't that bad, or Walter Peebles would've notified me. Or Jonathan.''

"Who's Jonathan?'' Spring queried, to which Chad gave a disbelieving glance.

"Jonathan Feathers? The senior partner in my law firm.''

"Oh, Mr. Feathers doesn't know anything about

it," Honor said. "And we begged Uncle Walter not to contact you. You couldn't have done anything without coming home, and we didn't feel we should interrupt your trip. Besides, Spring and I wanted to take care of ourselves. And we have."

Chad's features settled into angry, stubborn lines. His stare caught Spring's in a glacier mass. She wondered if he thought she was responsible for the entire series of events. Or, that she'd taken advantage of them for her own gain?

"Well, I'm home now," he said on a hard note, "and I'll take care of the finances and Honor's allowance. No more outside jobs, d'you hear? You won't need the money any longer. Or, at least, Honor won't."

"But, Chad, I like baby-sitting," Honor protested, her fist on a hip. "I'm good at it. And Spring and I are gaining a reputation by sitting as a team. The kids like us, and the parents like us even more. We've even sat for Mr. and Mrs. Peebles."

Chad groaned and closed his eyes. "Oh, great! I really needed to hear that…"

Spring added hastily, "We weren't unsafe, if that's what worries you. They sent us home in a cab, although it wasn't late. Lester was kind enough to wait up to see that we got into the building safely."

Eyes flashing like roman candles, Chad opened his mouth as though he wanted to swear roundly, but with one look at Honor's gaze, both pleading and puzzled, clamped it tightly closed and drummed his fingers on the table.

"All right," he muttered through his teeth. "I'll talk to Walter first thing in the morning and get a few things straightened out. Go to bed, now, pet. I want to talk to Spring alone."

"I don't think that's fair, Chad." Honor tossed her long dark braid behind her shoulder. "Spring's my friend and I—"

"Whether it's fair or not, go to bed!"

"It's all right, Honor." Spring laid a consoling hand on the girl's arm. "Perhaps you should go on to bed. You have that math final first thing tomorrow and need to sleep. Nothing drastic is going to happen tonight. We'll smooth things out."

"Chad?" Honor's gaze implored his compliance.

"Okay, okay. I promise I won't clobber your friend here, or eat her alive."

Honor visibly relaxed and let out a sudden giggle, dimples flashing. "Okay. But you won't fire her or anything, will you? Please?"

Chad took a deep breath and swung his chair away from the table before answering. "I won't take any action concerning Spring without discussing it with you first, is that all right? Now will you go to bed?"

Still, Honor hesitated, and he added, "We'll let you know in the morning if there's any change in the current, uh, living arrangements."

"Well, I think I should have a vote in what that is. In what happens now."

Chad seemed to gather whatever remnants of patience he had left as he answered one last argument. "I've heard your vote, Honor. I'll consider the matter from your viewpoint as well as my own, I double promise you, okay? Now scoot."

Spring turned her back and finished wiping the counter. After stacking the teacups into the small dishwasher, she closed the door and listened to Honor's footsteps fade. Behind her, Chad rose, and she glanced over her shoulder.

No longer angry, he appeared only exhausted.

"I'm going to take a quick shower and change. Do you mind staying up a while longer so we can have our little chat?"

"Of course not," she agreed. "But are you sure you're up to it? I mean, we can talk tomorrow morning just as well."

"I'd rather not put it off. I'll meet you in the living room in twenty minutes or so."

Spring waited as instructed, curled up in a deep chocolate-colored leather chair. The twenty minutes stretched to thirty, then forty.

She was ready for sleep, too, she thought, and yawned. A morning person, she usually turned in when Honor did.

He reappeared finally, wearing cutoff sweats. His hair was still damp. It was nearing midnight, and he hadn't bothered to shave.

Her first thought was that he appeared far less formidable in a more relaxed state. Then her heartbeat picked up ten paces, and she changed her mind. Masculine and sexy, his broad chest and strong arms showed a body used to regular workouts, and he'd been somewhere recently to maintain a healthy tan.

She felt a bit wary at her own response, and hugged a bright melon-hued pillow against her chest.

He let out a gusty sigh as he sat down on the leather couch, leaned back, and simply stared at her for a long moment. She felt the force of his gaze all through her body.

It was all she could do to sit still and remain silent.

"All right," he said finally, and leaned forward, resting his elbows on his knees.

The red pillow became a real shield. She tugged at its corners.

"I've checked with Walter. He's happy with your references, and since he knows this minister and his wife that you and Honor think walk with the angels, I'm willing to let you stay on in the capacity of housekeeper. For a while. If things work out, maybe we can come to a more permanent agreement. But I still have questions…"

"That's fair enough. Fire away."

"How long have you been in New York?"

"Not quite three months. I came in April."

"What brought you here? Job? Family? Ambition?"

"Oh, I guess you could say all three." Her fingers became more sensitive to the pillow stitching, and she imprinted the corner against them. "I want to study dress design with a lead designer if I can, and perhaps go on to Paris someday. Even Italy, maybe. But New York..." She waved a hand, letting her excitement show. "Oh, I just wanted to spend time here. I love American designers, and sure hope to find a niche with one. For a year or two, anyway."

She dared to meet his gaze momentarily, wondering what lay beyond the tired depths, wondering how much he was really interested in hearing of her plans. But he didn't interrupt, and she didn't know what to do but keep on chattering.

"But it's hard to get a decent appointment, you know? Oh, I could get a job as support personnel, I suppose, and maybe I'd be smart to do that, get my foot in the door and all that. But I'd like to find someplace where they appreciate my designs, too. Where they'll give me a chance."

Glimpsing his face, she abruptly hushed. He drew a deep breath.

"Okay... And you did say 'family'? You have family in New York?"

"No. I mean, I have family. A twin sister, Autumn. But not in New York. She lives in Kansas City. She, um, didn't want to come."

"I don't follow. Why would that bring you to New York?"

"Well, you see, Autumn and I have never lived apart. Except for a few minor choices, we've always done things as a twosome and rarely been separated.

We thought it time for each of us to, uh, sorta find our own identity.''

"And you had to come to New York to do that? Wasn't that a little drastic?''

"Mmm, my goodness, yes. Er, no, not drastic in that sense. But I have a better chance at finding my place in the design world here, and Autumn's a hometown girl through and through.''

He looked a little weary.

"Got that. But why would a young single woman, who's after a career of any kind, want to hire on as a housekeeper, of all things? Away from the singles' scene. And further, with the limitations and responsibility that looking after a young girl would bring? I'd think it would cramp your...ambitions.''

"Well, not all that much. I mean, I don't feel confined. Not yet, anyway. We've had too much fun doing the tourist thing to hurry, both of us being new to the city. I haven't pushed it. Up until now...well, I've had time during the day to make a few rounds while Honor attends school. But lately we've been talking about summer plans, and that will change our routine.''

She glanced at him with sudden inquisitiveness. "You do know she completes her classes this week? The private school is on a little different schedule than the public system.''

"Actually, that's one thing I did know. That's the main reason I returned early.''

"Oh.''

"So tell me, Spring. How and why did you take the job here? If you moved to get away from always pairing with your sister, haven't you merely changed the person and the locale if you and Honor are always together?"

"It really isn't the same. I am nine years older than Honor, and we aren't viewed as a set. Here, there's only one of me."

"Ah, I see. Well, what is this bargain you and Honor Suzanne have both mentioned?"

"Oh, that." She traced the pillow stitching, back and forth. "As you must know, New York apartments are very expensive, and while my Uncle William left me enough money to live modestly for a year or two without worry, he also taught Autumn and me to live rather frugally when we could and not to squander money."

He raised a brow. "The point being?"

"So, when I began attending the church, I thought it would be a good place to find a roommate. I didn't want to just pick someone from the ads or anything, you know—that's not always safe in New York these days, is it? Anywhere at all, I suppose. Then Dana and I began to talk, and she introduced me to Honor."

"And?"

"We made our bargain. I'd be her companion and resident adult, and in exchange, I live here rent-free. We pooled our resources for food and other cash demands."

"But if Honor wasn't getting her allowance, what cash resources did she have?"

"Oh, we told you that. Baby-sitting and other odd jobs."

"Ah, yes, the baby-sitting…"

"And the other things. Like organizing and running that birthday party for the busy mother. You know, that could become quite a nice little business, if you ask me. Honor and I have been talking—"

"Oh, no, you don't." He put up a hand, palm out, and leaned against the couch once more. "I don't want my home turned into a business center. Besides, you can't, remember? No business may be run from this complex."

"That's a shame. We could—"

"Whatever you wish, Spring, it won't happen here."

Spring sighed. "All right."

"Now we need to come to a better agreement over your terms of employment."

"My terms of employment?"

"Yes. If you are to remain in this apartment as housekeeper and Honor's…uh, helper companion, we have to have a firm understanding about what to expect from each other, don't you agree?"

Spring had thought she and Honor were more friends than housekeeper and charge. At home, she and Autumn had shared household chores, although she'd been the shopper for household goods and groceries. It seemed only a little different between her and Honor—except she'd been teaching Honor to cook and they were learning New York ways together. But she hadn't felt like an employee.

Still, she had free rent here, and in an excellent neighborhood. She loved Honor, and they had a growing bond in the excursions they did together, especially the Bible studies on Sunday evenings at the church. They were opening her mind as nothing else ever had. The church was only a few blocks away, and easy to reach. She liked her situation here.

How much could possibly change by Chad being at home, too? He'd merely be another person to rotate a schedule around, to prepare a meal for. And if she and Autumn could accommodate the finicky eating habits of Uncle William and his need for a spotless house, she supposed she could meet Chad's requirements. Would being tagged a "housekeeper" really make that much difference?

"Well…"

"Yes?"

"Honor and I share the household chores now, plus the shopping and cooking. I usually run any other errands during the day, but I have used much of the time Honor is in school to make my rounds of the design houses and such. I wouldn't want to lose that freedom."

"Mmm… As I say, we'll have to see how all that works out, won't we? Now, you will be compensated for your time. Would the salary I offered Mrs. Hinkle be sufficient?"

Spring gasped. "More than enough. I'm not sure…"

"But without the need to earn extra money—" he said it as though it left a sour taste in his mouth "—you'll have more time to take care of the apartment, now doesn't that make sense?"

"Yes, of course, but I'd keep the apartment clean regardless, you see. And as I've said, Honor and I share the chores." She grinned and tossed out, "She actually likes dusting."

He returned her glance with one of skepticism, then firmed his mouth.

"You'd better accept what I offer, Spring, or move on. I'm inclined to be generous in view of your picking up after the mess left by Mrs. Hinkle. And your very kind, extended involvement with Honor Suzanne's needs. Walter speaks highly of your efforts."

"That's nice of Mr. Peebles to say. But Honor and I are friends, Mr. Alexander." She couldn't prevent her hurt from showing, though she made a valiant effort to speak evenly. "Whatever I've done for Honor, I did from that starting point. I don't need payment for it."

"I didn't intend an insult…" He ran a hand through his already tousled hair. "Boy, I'm tired. What I mean to say is, you stepped into a sticky situation, from what Walter tells me, and I recognize—"

"Let's just call it even for now, Mr. Alexander."

"All right. For now. But if we're to share the apartment on, um, these terms, you must call me Chad."

"Yes, that makes sense. And you are exactly right, Chad. We must see how we all get along before we reach a permanent agreement," she added and stood. "You can put your money into a household account for Honor and me to draw on, and I'll keep a running account so that you'll know where it's being spent. Then I'll take, say a couple or three morning hours a week for myself, and you won't even miss me. Honor and I can stay on our routine, and you can let us know when you'll be home for dinner. So how about a month's trial for all of us?"

Five minutes later, Chad stood in his bedroom, staring at the neatly made bed as he ran a hand against his unshaven jaw, wondering just what it was he'd been caught up in. Just how on God's green earth had he lost control of his personal living situation? Of his *own* apartment?

Chapter Four

From his office the following morning, Chad contacted a first-class private investigator. Walter Peebles had suggested he take the matter to John Allen, of Allen and Parker, a discreet firm his colleagues had used a time or two.

"I don't have an investigator in Kansas City, so it will take a day or two to find someone. Or else send a man out there to do a proper job." John's deep voice rumbled as he spoke. "Even with the Internet, faxes and phones, it's better to do personal background checks, to the depth you're wanting, in the geographical location where a person lives."

"Fine. That's fine," Chad muttered. "Just get it done as fast as possible. I don't want any delays that can be avoided. This young woman is already living in my home."

"I'll have someone on it no later than this afternoon, Mr. Alexander,'' John soothed. ''Before we're through, we'll know the girl's dress size, her favorite music, food and color, and how many boyfriends she had in the fourth grade. If there's anything in her background that doesn't spell squeaky clean, we'll find it.''

''I'll wait for your call.'' Chad hung up and rested against his high-backed chair, his hands laced behind his head. His thick, overgrown hair brushed over his hands, and the thought passed through his mind to get it cut this morning. If he could make the time.

Swiveling, he stared out of the twenty-fourth floor window at New York's skyline. He'd been impressed with his view from the moment he moved into this space, and proud to be a part of New York's unique society.

Though oddly, he hadn't missed this sight while in Europe nearly as much as anticipated, he thought now, and it had no power to soothe him this morning. He still felt unsettled.

Flexing his tight shoulder muscles, he pushed that thought aside. Analyzing his reactions could wait. He'd come home to more pressing matters. He'd had to take care of his own personal needs before he began on his workday.

He hadn't stopped thinking about Spring, or his newly challenged home situation, all morning.

Rising earlier than normal, he'd discovered he hadn't been early enough to avoid signs of his new housekeeper. A full pot of freshly ground and steaming coffee waited for him in the kitchen at six-thirty. The *New York Times,* untouched and pristine, lay on the tiny table. Alongside the paper were two boxes of cereal, both sugarless, and a bowl, spoon and a banana lay upon a cherry-red place mat.

He saw nothing of Spring. That she'd anticipated his breakfast needs startled and annoyed him at the same time. It all smacked of a too-perfect picture, and his suspicions notched even higher. But if he'd hoped to pretend his life was still his own, that breakfast layout had put it to a speedy end.

He'd taken his coffee and ignored the banana and cereal.

His reverie tumbled when Anne Martin, his personal assistant, came bustling in and set a cup of coffee, strong and black, beside his hand. He'd come into the office early to get a jump start on his day before most of the staff came in, and a good piece of that had flown out the window. Irritated with himself for dawdling, he twirled back to face his desk. Work waited.

"Welcome back, Chad. Glad you're home early. The office wasn't the same without you," Anne told him brightly. Anne, a well-groomed brunette in her thirties, tossed him a concerned glance.

"Thanks." He shuffled through a pile of catch-up work that would take him about a week to plow through, matters that only he could handle within the firm. He may as well get started.

"You look like...well—" she frowned "—you don't look as though you've had much rest."

"No, I haven't. Long flight and only a few hours' sleep." He shrugged and took the list Anne handed him. The list, from Jonathan Feathers, the senior partner of the firm, contained things that needed his immediate attention. "What's up?"

"Lots." Anne took a chair facing him, causing him to look up. She never sat unless she had something serious to say. "I'm sorry to be the one to tell you this, Chad, but we've been in somewhat of a tizzy this week."

He leaned back in his chair once more and gave her his full attention. "Okay, shoot."

"Jonathan had a gall bladder attack and has been out of the loop."

"Is he all right?"

"For the moment—but he may face surgery. He's resting at home." She took a deep breath. "And old Dale died suddenly two days ago. Half the staff is leaving at noon to attend his funeral in Connecticut. Jonathan already knows you're back. He wants you to attend if you possibly can."

Chad bit back his first reaction; Jonathan being out of the office just as he returned put a double load on everyone. And now a death?

"Old Dale?" He'd been rather fond of old Dale, a longtime staffer, even though they'd had little in common and their paths seldom crossed. "Well, I'm very sorry to hear it, and we'll miss him, but it's not all that sudden, surely? His heart had been failing. How's his wife doing? The funeral's today, is it?''

"Yes, today. At two-thirty. And Tillie is okay, but…''

Anne continued to fill him in on everything going on in the firm, down to the engagement of their new receptionist. He gave her his usual concentrated attention, pulling out the nuggets that concerned him most, and took notes of what, if anything, he should do about them. He then gave her a few directions of his own to follow.

After she'd gone, he settled back to prioritize his day. The long drive to Connecticut for the funeral would take most of it.

He called the garage where his car was stored and arranged for it to be readied. It hadn't been used in the weeks he'd been gone.

When he'd done that, he found himself gazing out the window once more. He'd brought home a lot of business with his European contacts, and the firm, Feathers, Sanders, Sanders & Alexander, was set to grow. It was a bad time to lose old Dale. They'd have to hire someone to take the old man's place as soon as possible. He wondered why Walter Peebles hadn't mentioned the loss last night.

Yet Walter wasn't an insider with the firm, and last night, his own concerns had been strictly personal. Walter had been his father's friend and accountant, older than Chad by a dozen years. Chad had used Walter's expertise a lot these past six months since his dad's death. Walter had been a big help in finding Honor Suzanne's private school, as well, after she'd refused to remain at the boarding school to which he'd first sent her.

Chad trusted Walter's judgment about most things. And Walter had insisted he had nothing to worry about in Spring. Yet he simply couldn't let it stand without further investigation.

"You can do as you please," Walter had told him last night, "but I think you'll find my opinion supported, Chad. Spring Barbour is as solid and sound as she appears. Nothing about her to alarm anyone."

"That's easy for you to say, Walter. You aren't allowing an unknown girl to take complete charge of your household. We don't know what kind of behavior she's capable of, or what's in her past."

"Well, going through the employment agency didn't insure you against an unscrupulous woman, now did it?"

"That's another matter, Walter. That agency has a lot to answer for, and I intend to take it up with them first thing in the morning. But this girl came here out of the blue. I need to know more about her."

"Do as you see fit, Chad, but I'll bet you my tickets to the next Yankees game that she's as clean and as sweet as she seems. No drugs or wild behavior for her."

"That's just it, Walter. The girl seems altogether too picture perfect to be true. I don't think such a woman exists in this day and age. What's her angle?''

''No angle, other than she needed a place to live while she gets her feet wet. This city takes some getting used to for out-of-towners, Chad, don't you remember? But you got it right the first time. A girl, that's what Spring still is—not yet a woman, if you know what I mean. The worst thing you can say about Spring is she's naive and too innocent for her age. You might want to watch that. But that isn't all bad, pal. She makes a great little chum for Honor Suzanne.''

''I suppose you could have a point,'' he'd responded slowly. He hadn't been ready to give up his objections against the situation thrust on him, even while he realized he had little choice at the moment.

He didn't like losing control. He liked being in charge, making his own choices.

''And a blessed good point,'' Walter continued, ''but I have to say that my Libby is the one who made it. Chad, you must know your father kept Honor Suzanne on a rather tight leash after Sandra died. The girl needs young company. She needs more friends her age, someone to help her be a teenager at the right time of her life. She needs to go places, and do the teenage thing, you know what I mean? I think Spring's a good one to help her do that.''

That was the point at which he'd thanked Walter and said good-night.

Now Chad thought that waiting over the next few days for the investigative report on Spring was going to demand more of his energy and patience than he'd like. A lot more.

Running a hand across his forehead, he pulled the stack of case files Anne said needed his immediate attention toward him. He might get a little work done before he left for the funeral.

Spring spent the day cleaning and making sure everything in the apartment sparkled. Flicking a last particle of dust from a lamp, she gazed around the sunny living room, noting how the rather austere furniture looked so much cozier with the few bright pillows she'd added.

Chad hadn't said a word last night about the way she and Honor had brightened the apartment. They'd had to do something with the drab decor, they'd both agreed. Perhaps Chad was the kind of man who didn't notice such things. Or care.

She hadn't planned to spend the morning cleaning; before Chad came home, she'd actually planned on making a call on two small design houses that Dana had suggested. And in the months she'd been in New York, she had yet to approach any of the design schools for an application.

She pushed that idea aside. She had time, and she wasn't sure she honestly wanted to attend any of them yet, rationalizing it was because she wanted to be creatively free to do her own thinking. That she felt a bit intimidated by the whole idea, she wouldn't allow into her thoughts.

Under the circumstances, she supposed she was lucky not to be out apartment hunting.

Facing Chad had been far more nerve-wracking than she'd anticipated, although she'd known it would come. What she'd expected, she wasn't now sure of, but it wasn't...Chad.

His disconcerting stares had run through her like the rising tide, leaving a mini-wake along her veins as it settled. If it really had settled. She wasn't sure. How they would get along on a day-to-day existence remained to be seen, but if he continued to look at her the way he had, she was likely to turn blue with holding her breath. Perhaps his odd effect on her would wear off in time.

Uh-huh. And she was likely to be invited to dinner at Trump Towers.

Twirling away from the dining room, she giggled and set a CD to play. It was too late to make any kind of business rounds today. Perhaps, since Honor would be completing her math finals, Spring would bake a pie to celebrate, instead.

She liked baking pies. Her thoughts often did their most creative design work while her hands were otherwise occupied. She'd come up with a lovely idea for a summer suit just yesterday, and was eager to buy some lightweight fabric to make it up.

Sighing, she realized that would now have to wait. Her personal activities had to be curtailed and arranged around her daily housekeeping chores. She wouldn't have as much time to follow through with her own plans.

Ah, well. There were worse things than living on New York's upper east side and making a salary, while looking for the ideal job. At least Uncle William's exacting demands for a spotless house would not go to waste. She and Autumn had learned to clean, cook and sew with the best little *Good Housekeeping* examples Uncle William could find. She could recall his often repeated words as though he said them at her shoulder now: *"A disordered home denotes a disordered life."*

She smiled. Uncle William would approve of her. She'd been smart and frugal with her funds, and hadn't had to spend much of her small inheritance.

But she sincerely hoped Chad had no occasion to peek into her bedroom. It was a shambles, with stacks of fabric and sewing debris piled wherever she'd found available space. Her main task there was to at least keep the pins off the floor to prevent injury to her bare feet.

Or she needed to remember to put on her shoes.

The quiet ring of the phone caught her just as she slid the pie into the oven. She'd taken a couple of messages for Chad already today—female voices, sounding young and sophisticated, or savvy and businesslike, asking to have Chad return their calls. Spring had taken several such calls when she first took up residence with Honor, but over the passing weeks the calls had slowed and stopped.

News of Chad's return had rocketed now, she thought in amusement as she grabbed the kitchen extension.

"This is Chad," he said in return to her hello, then proceeded to give her directions with a firm, instructional tone. "I've arranged for a household account for anything you or Honor may need, and opened up a couple of charge cards for Honor at Macy's, Bloomingdale's and a couple of other places. Did you find the cash I left on the kitchen counter for groceries?"

"Yes, as a matter of fact, I did. Thanks, I'll restock the cupboards and fridge. Is there anything particular you'd like for dinner?"

"Don't think I'll make it home for dinner. Sorry."

"Oh. Well, is there a message for Honor?"

"Um, no, I...just tell my sister to follow her usual routine. I'll stop into her room to say good-night before going to bed."

"All right. Chad?"

"Yes?"

"Honor would like to enroll in a summer ballet class, if it's all right with you."

"Sure. Why shouldn't it be?"

"Well, it runs through August. I didn't know what your summer plans may be."

"Plans?" He sounded distracted.

"Many people don't like to be tied down through

the summer months," she explained. "If you have family vacation plans, it may interfere."

"Ah." He'd caught her direction, but his immediate "No, I don't have any further plans for the summer" put an end to her hope that he'd take a week or so to spend with Honor. The girl needed her brother's company, in Spring's opinion. She'd noticed too many lost, plaintive expressions on the child's face while Honor had thought herself unobserved.

"If she wants to join the class," he went on quickly, giving her the feeling he was in a hurry to wrap up the conversation, "it's fine with me. Whatever equipment or clothing she needs, use the charge cards. I'll discuss it more fully later, all right?"

"Yes, of course, I only thought—" But he was gone before she could voice her thoughts.

She sighed, picked up a stack of bills lying beneath the phone, then set them down again. They were no longer her worry.

Glancing at her watch, she realized Honor would be home soon. She made up her mind. Since Chad wouldn't be home until late, why shouldn't she take Honor to register this very afternoon? Then they could buy what Honor needed for the class, find a bite to eat, and run straight on to the Wednesday night teen gathering at church. She could deliver the finished dress to her customer Mary Beth, on the way.

But she wasn't about to tell Mary Beth that this

was the last sewing she could do for her. Chad couldn't dictate whom she sewed for, and if he didn't know she was being paid for it, he couldn't object.

Chapter Five

Well after nine o'clock, Chad drummed his fingers along his leather chair arm while he valiantly tried to keep his attention on a repeat of a boring TV comedy. Being stressed out wasn't how he'd pictured his evening, on his long drive home from Connecticut. After the demanding, intense day, he'd simply wanted to come home and relax. Read a couple of case studies on the new businesses he'd brought home from Europe, and go to bed early. After all, he still felt short of sleep.

Only, the apartment had been empty when he'd expected to find two giggling, chattering girls. Or at least one of them practicing a ballet twirl. It was too quiet for comfort. Not even the TV had been on.

Faced with all that silence, he hadn't been able to get beyond taking a quick shower and planting himself down in the living room. Oh, he'd taken his files out of his briefcase. He'd even shuffled through a few papers, but it was no use. He couldn't concentrate.

Where were they? What were they doing? His mind leapt to a hundred possibilities, most of them filled with possible dangers for two very innocent girls in the big city.

When he finally heard a key in the front door, Chad glanced at his watch for the tenth time in thirty minutes. *It's about time,* he mentally muttered as two low feminine murmurs reached his ears. He pushed out of his chair; his stride lengthened as he headed their way. He rounded the living room corner into the entry hall just in time to catch a huge yawn on Honor's face.

"Where on God's green earth have you two been? Do you know what time it is?"

"Um, about a quarter to ten?" Spring answered, giving him a questioning gaze. "What's the matter?"

"Matter? You tell me. Where were you?"

"Don't get all bent outa shape, Chad," Honor answered. "We only went to the teen Bible Study."

"A Bible study?" he scoffed. "On a school night?"

"So?" Honor shrugged, giving him a puzzled I-can't-believe-this-is-a-problem stare. She moved past him into the living room, where she set a scuffed, leather-bound Bible on the end table. "It's Wednesday."

Chad turned to follow. His sister spoke as though he should understand completely with that bit of casual information. As though Wednesday held an aura all its own.

"What's Wednesday got to do with it? I expected you to be home hours ago on a school night. Studying and into bed at a decent hour." He turned to Spring as she came into the larger space. "Is this how it's been? You let her stay out as late as she wants, baby-sitting till all hours and whatever...running the streets?"

"We're not 'running the streets,' Chad. We're only doing wholesome activities. Stuff that most teens do. And if Honor needed more sleep than she does, I'd probably see that we're home earlier on a school night. But she does just fine on the mornings after we're out."

"What about homework?" He pursed his mouth, irritated and feeling like his old set-in-his-ways grandfather, yet unable to help himself. He was responsible for a growing young girl now, and it was up to him to monitor her activities. Spring should know that.

"I've done my homework. And it's not even ten," Honor protested, but then her voice softened. "Don't be upset, Chad. It's a common night for midweek Bible study and prayer. Families often go there together."

"Well, you might've told me."

"We didn't expect you to be home yet," Spring

answered in a conciliatory tone. "You said you had business matters to see to and would return late."

"I didn't know what time I'd get home, but..." He rubbed a thumb against his temple. The funeral had proved more involved and emotional for some of the office personnel than expected, and as the partner representing Jonathan Feathers, he'd stayed longer than planned to offer the widow his assistance. "Well, at least you're home," he mumbled grudgingly, "You can go right to—"

"Uh-huh." Honor headed toward the kitchen. "What did you buy at the store today, Spring? I'm starved."

"—bed," he finished under his breath as he realized Honor was ignoring him.

"There's fruit in the fridge," Spring said, her eyes flashing with humor as she followed Honor. She barely covered a grin. "And some light cottage cheese."

"It's a good thing we had burgers and fries before," Honor grumbled, her head already in the refrigerator by the time Chad paused in the kitchen door. "Isn't it a well-known fact that teens need lots of junk food?"

"Cottage cheese is food," Spring protested.

"In whose opinion?" Honor shot back.

"Well, I suppose you could have a tiny slice of the apple pie I baked this morning," Spring conceded. "In honor of your passing your math final."

"You baked an apple pie?" Chad asked, a bit incredulously.

"Yummy!" Honor swung the fridge door closed. "How did you know I'd pass my final?"

"Oh, I had faith you would," Spring returned. She reached for a plastic keeper sitting on the counter corner. She lifted the pie out, set it on the table and reached for plates, while Honor scrambled for forks. Glancing Chad's way, she said, "I'm surprised you didn't find it."

"I...didn't even think..." He'd found cheese and crackers earlier, but he hadn't thought to look in that container.

His stomach clutched in hunger as he stared at the golden-brown crust. It looked as good as any offered in one of New York's finest bakeries. Better. All his jumbled worries of the day seemed to dissolve as he eagerly scooted his chair out and accepted the generous cut Spring handed him.

"Mmm..." Honor let her appreciation be known past a mouthful of pastry. "Is this the kind of temptation into sin we're supposed to guard against?"

"Do you mean gluttony?" Spring asked, a mischievous smile edging the corner of her mouth. "Should I stop making these?"

"Not on your life!" Honor mumbled.

"Well, I wouldn't want to be the cause of your downfall."

"I think it's all right if we don't indulge beyond reason," Honor said on a highly contented sigh.

"That would be gluttony. But Josh said something tonight I've been thinking about."

"What's that?"

"The easy way it sneaks up on you. Temptation, I mean. I know he was talking about the drug and alcohol thing, about how it's easy to follow your friends when you think they're cool and they're doing cool things. Getting into sex is a really big thing for lots of kids, too. But he meant more than that, didn't he?"

"Yeah, I'd say that," Spring agreed. She glanced at Chad, her gaze questioning his thoughts on the subject. "It happens in little ways we don't expect."

"Uh-huh. Like when I lost my temper with Shanna, at school today. Honestly, she ticks me off on purpose. She's such a know-everything snot. But it didn't make it better when I mouthed back at her."

"Who's Shanna?" Chad asked. He'd listened and watched with interest as the teasing byplay between Spring and Honor turned serious. He was beginning to understand how little he knew of his sister's life. "Is she a friend?"

"No way! She's a pest."

"Another student, hmm?" He gave his sister a sympathetic glance.

"I wish! If she was, I could handle her. But—" Honor swallowed another bite of pie and sighed. "She's the school librarian, and this is her first job. She's not any older than you, Spring, but she's so full of herself and know-it-all. If I do one thing that doesn't line up with her list of rules, she makes a federal case out of it.''

"Well, the school year is almost over," Spring said. "You have only a few more days to put up with her rules."

Honor grinned. "Yeah, but her stupid rules lead me into temptation something fierce. Like she caught me taking three reference books down at one time, and I dropped one. She wants us to take only one at a time from the shelves, and she went on and on about how expensive the books were and how we needed to take better care of them. And we mustn't talk, we mustn't disturb the sanctity of library tradition. Those references will be on computer any year now, so I don't see what all the fuss is about. But she made me want to climb on a table right there and then and sing at the top of my voice just for spite, when before I wouldn't have given such an idea a thought.''

Chad burst out laughing. The account sounded so much like his own attitude during his teen years. "But you didn't do that, did you?"

Honor made a face. "'Course not. I don't want to get thrown out of school! But I was tempted…" She carried her plate to the sink, rinsed it and put it into the dishwasher. "Now I'm ready for bed, Chad.''

His sister bent and kissed his cheek. Her affection warmed him, gave him a feeling of rare bonding. They hadn't had much of that at all in the past. Guilt grabbed his heart. His fault, he knew. He hadn't spent much time visiting the family home in Virginia.

Chad watched his sister go before turning his eyes toward Spring. "She's so young. She hasn't a clue what real temptation is yet."

"Oh, I don't know about that," Spring returned on a soft note.

"I don't think I was ever that young," he insisted.

Spring's gaze grew speculative. "Being young holds no barrier against the daily temptations in life, Chad. She's young, I'll agree, but she's been through quite a lot with the loss of both parents. That teaches a bushel of lessons. In some ways, I think Honor's running in ancient time, and only fourteen on paper."

Chad laid his fork across his plate. "Tell me about this church. How did Spring become interested in attending it?"

"Oh, that's an easy one to answer. She is looking for something solid and unshifting in her life. Her faith in God offers that. She remembers going to church with your mom and dad. Evidently, they were a big part of a congregation where they lived in Virginia, before your parents died."

"Sandra was Honor's mother, but not mine," Chad muttered in a flat tone. He couldn't keep his fingers still, rearranging the fork on the plate and picking up pastry crumbs. "And I scarcely recall my father ever attending church. He wouldn't go when my mother was alive."

"Oh...well..." Spring shot him a curious, sympathetic glance. Her blue-green eyes held flecks of mixed emotion, like turquoise yet unmined. He fleetingly wondered what it would take to reap it from its half-hidden depths.

"Mr. Peebles directed Honor there," Spring went on, "and she loves this church. We both do, actually, and I didn't go to church much as a child, either. I'm beginning to understand how much Autumn and I missed out on by not having a church family."

"I suppose a social need is readily fulfilled by churches," Chad remarked, and rose.

"Social needs?" Spring looked surprised. "Yes, that's true enough, I suppose. I'll admit that's why I first attended. To find friends and help during those first weeks in the city."

She paused in gathering the dirty dishes from the table, then added slowly, "But that's not why I keep going. It's more than an institution, I'm finding. Every time I hear Josh Nolan speak, or the senior pastor Claude Bates, something in me hears a truth I didn't know before. Sunday mornings, with the music and worship..." She shook her head as she placed the dishes on the counter beside the sink. "Something or Someone Beyond speaks to me."

Her eyes engaged his, open and questing and seeking a response. It struck him that she sometimes seemed as young as his sister. That's what Walter had implied, as well.

Only her softening mouth didn't affect him like a

sister's; it sent shock waves of awareness through the pit of his stomach. His natural desire was to reach out and touch her bottom lip....

The temptation to kiss those lips hit him like a bat connecting with a ball, and he jerked his thoughts away from that direction.

She feels things strongly, as Honor does, Chad thought. As *young* Honor does. Was Spring really a whole nine years older than his sister?

Eleven years younger than me, he reminded himself. Mentally, he stepped back a pace. He hadn't had a chance to get a proper report on Spring yet, but if she was an actress or a con, she was certainly a good one. But he did wonder just how much maturity he could count on from her.

"Perhaps I should go along the next time you two go to church," he said, moving past her and out of the kitchen. "That way I'll know what you two are talking about."

And what they were really doing.

He said goodnight and settled himself in the living room once more. This time he picked up his folders for real. He half listened to the television news, finished going over his schedule for the next few days, made a few notes for the office, and finally, close to midnight, turned out the living room lights.

A huge yawn stretched his mouth wide. He was exhausted. He'd run short of sleep for the last week.

The apartment had grown quiet, but he heard a low hum start and stop as he passed Spring's door.

He paused, puzzled at the faint clipping sounds that followed. The girl must be a busy little night owl, he guessed. Too tired, he shrugged and let out a deep sigh. No need to immediately solve the particular little mystery of what she was doing. It could wait till morning. He didn't understand why he should even want to know.

His own door was half-open when Spring swung hers free behind him. She glanced over his shoulder as she stepped into the hall. A light summer robe patterned with bright blue flowers swished about her bare toes as she came to an abrupt halt. "Oh! It's you…"

"Did you expect someone else?" He kept his voice and irritation low. It wasn't her fault he felt invaded.

"Yes—er, no, of course not," she responded in a whisper, glancing at his sister's closed door. A night-light near the floor gave soft shadows to her face, but her eyes appeared luminous. "It's only that I heard a noise, and I thought maybe Honor might need me."

"In the middle of the night?"

"Well, sometimes…" She brushed her wispy bangs from her eyes. Her hesitation was so obvious, he felt like shaking her. What was there to hide?

"Go on. What is it?"

"She, um…still cries…"

"Cries?" He felt stunned, and caught his breath. His sister cried in the night? Why hadn't he known?

Spring bit her lip, then seemed to make up her mind. She reached out to touch his arm, then beckoned him to follow as she glided back into the living room. There, she perched on the arm of the sofa, and he stopped only a few feet from her. He didn't turn on a lamp, and only the hall night-light gave them a glow. As high as their apartment was, little light shone from beyond the windows.

He could barely make out the lines of Spring's face, and the tips of her long lashes as she gazed up at him. Yet her concern came to him in a wave of earnestness.

"Chad, you must realize Honor is still grieving the loss of her dad. They were so close, don't you see? Especially after her mother died only two years ago."

"Ah, I see… Yes—yes, of course." He shoved his hands in his pockets and stared at his feet. Putting a loafered heel to toe, he measured his steps as he made a tight little circle, thinking hard.

"I thought that she *would* miss Dad, of course. I do, as well," he said, coming to a stop in front of her. "But I've been on my own for more than a dozen years and I'm used to my own schedules. My own life. That's why I enrolled Honor in that boarding school so soon after. She's such a spunky kid, I thought she'd find companions there and other girls growing up without the daily family gathering thing. But she hated it."

"Mmm-hmm. She told me all about it when we first became acquainted."

He nodded. He felt nagged with failure. Finding the right solutions for a sibling's needs hadn't been a part of his training.

"After that one didn't work, Walter Peebles helped me find the school she's in now." He met her eyes. "She didn't complain."

"Honor does a good job of hiding behind her spunky I-am-woman-hear-me-roar shield," Spring said with a nod. "Only a couple of months in a new school, even a school you like, is hardly enough time to feel established and…at home."

"And I left for Europe soon afterward." He made his statement in a quiet way, yet he felt totally convicted of his careless consideration of his young sister. She must have felt completely abandoned. Well, he'd have to make some changes beyond just the obvious ones, he supposed. Spend more time with Honor. Make New York feel like her home.

"Is she still homesick for Virginia?"

"Sometimes," Spring admitted, then added, "Often."

"How often has she had nights…well, bouts of grieving?"

"A few times right after I first moved in. Not as much lately, though. I talked with Dana Bates about it that first week. She seemed to think Honor only needed time to adjust and go through the natural grieving process. Keeping her too busy to feel lonely was a good plan, don't you think?''

"I suppose New York is a good place to do that."

"It could be the last place to do that."

"What do you mean? There's everything in the world to do here."

"But it doesn't mean anything if a person has to do those things alone. But don't worry. Honor and I are having a grand time exploring the city together. Lots of new experiences to grow up on. It's an adventure."

Adventure! New experiences! How many, not so innocent, might be found along the city streets? How many would he prefer his sister not to experience at all? What would someone older find exciting that his sister shouldn't?

He still wanted to see those reports on this young woman.

"Well, I think you'd better count on running your plans by me in the future," he stated with firm resolve. "There are some New York adventures I'd just as soon not expose Honor to, and there're a few I'd like to take charge of myself."

He turned to leave, then paused in the hall doorway. "And I'll be home everyday by seven or thereabouts from now on throughout the summer. We'll draw up a schedule of activities tomorrow."

"Yes, sir" came the soft reply just as he swung his door wide. "As you wish, sir."

Did he detect a humorous edge to her voice? A

mocking one? He couldn't be sure, but decided to let that one alone. Adjusting to two young females in his home was proving to be a real test of courage. Lord, he hoped—he prayed—he was up to it.

Chapter Six

A few days later, John Allen called just before noon, and Chad made arrangements to meet the investigator during his lunch hour at the corner deli closest to his office. John assured him there was nothing of alarm in his report, but Chad couldn't squelch his eagerness to see the report for himself.

Chad ordered a sandwich and cola at the deli, and sat down at a table to wait. John Allen strolled in a few minutes later, ordered coffee, then sat opposite and pulled a folder from his briefcase, which he placed in front of Chad.

"No police record—not even a traffic ticket," he said, lifting his cup to his lips for a long sip. "Neighbors liked her, former college instructor recalled her as normal, nothing about her to stand out from the class. Did her assignments on time, made good grades. Only place she ever worked, a fabric store, said she was a conscientious employee." He nodded toward the report. "The rest is there."

Chad swallowed a gulp of soda and opened the folder to read the neatly typed report, while his sandwich sat untouched.

Spring and Autumn Barbour were raised in Kansas City by an uncle, William. Their mother died when they were eight. Father left before that, whereabouts unknown. They attended public schools until sixth grade, then were home schooled.

"What happened then? Why did they stop going to public schools?" Chad asked, looking up.

"Our man couldn't find out, specifically," Allen answered. "Seems the uncle was unhappy over how the girls were treated or something, and took them out. After that, they had a few tutors who came to the house, but mostly old William taught them himself."

"I wonder why he just didn't place them in a private school," Chad muttered, thinking aloud.

"Former neighbors said William was old-fashionedly upright and a bit overprotective. Harmless, but…"

"Hmm?" Chad was reading again.

Community college, as she'd said. Then Spring had completed a general studies program at KCMU, continuing to live at home all the while. The sister didn't go in for formal classes except private studies in art.

Spring had never held a full-time job; her former

manager of the fabric store had said Spring was uninterested in retail as a career. And finally, Chad read that Spring occasionally dated a boy named Tyler Goth, also a student.

Chad looked up once more. How interested had Spring been in Tyler Goth? Surely there was more. This report read like a Girl Scout report.

"What is it?" He laid the report down and looked at John. "What's the 'but'?"

"These young women seem to have had a rather odd upbringing." John pointed his finger at page three. "Old-fashioned, at least. For instance, your young woman, Spring, seldom went out without her sister. Twins to the extreme, seems like, in some ways. Never dressed alike, didn't always have the same interests, the sister shy while this one is friendly and outgoing."

Chad leaned forward. It felt odd to have Spring referred to as "his young woman," but he shook that off in favor of asking, "And?"

Allen shook his head. "Terry, my man in Kansas City, said the neighbors had some interesting things to say about the family. They never took vacations. Seems Autumn has a phobia of some kind. Crowds, one neighbor said. That may account for the change in the school situation. Too many people in one place, and all that. In any case, up till a few months ago the sisters remained very close. They both occasionally dated, but usually together, and most of the time Spring set up the occasions. But now the sister is living alone and seems to get along okay.''

"What broke the pattern?" Chad asked.

"The uncle died at the end of last year. The twins sold the house at his instruction, according to one neighbor. Besides that, old William left them each with a bit of money. Autumn settled into a downtown loft apartment and Spring moved here to the Big Apple.''

Chad ruffled the papers in front of him. Spring had told him much of this, her telling done in a breezy, offhand style that disclaimed any possible melodrama. He hadn't really believed all of it, suspending his opinion while waiting for this report, thinking she surely couldn't have lived such an innocent, rather insular life.

Yet he had to admit the report didn't hold any real surprises, and it backed up Spring's claim to understand Honor's emotions. It didn't answer all his questions, though. Was she merely substituting Honor for her sister? Was she emotionally dependent on fulfilling another's needs?

Was she still in touch with her boyfriend Tyler?

Why should Chad care? Sure, Spring was as enticing as a wood nymph, a bit of an Audrey Hepburn sprite, but she wasn't his type. Never mind that a vivid image of her graceful figure moving to the music kept popping into his head at inappropriate times. She was much too young for him, anyway. He liked more sophisticated women: tall, leggy blondes.

He brought his thoughts to bear on how the report applied to his household. Would it be so bad to have a companion for Honor who liked the nurturing role? Whoever said such a woman needed to be older?

"Is that all?" he asked John Allen.

"That seems to be it."

Chad couldn't make up his mind whether he had really expected to hear something damaging about Spring. Certainly, he felt relieved to have the report. Spring was as open as the Sunday newspaper, easy to read and as fresh as new ink.

Chad thanked the investigator, directed that a bill be sent to his office, and they parted. He munched on his sandwich, in no hurry to return to work. He read through the report again, looking for anything he might have missed the first time through. Nothing alarming leapt to his attention.

So...it appeared that Spring Eve Barbour had been totally honest with him. He supposed that left him with two choices: either accept her completely at face value and admit his own prejudice in thinking her entirely too young and unsophisticated for his needs. His other choice was to continue to think she had a hidden agenda.

He couldn't imagine what that could be. He had nothing to offer an enterprising young designer.

And what were his own purposes, exactly? His needs? His requirements in a companion for Honor?

Walter had asked him that very question at one point in their discussion the night he arrived home.

Indeed, his first thoughts on the matter were to hire a woman who would run his household with little input from him, except that he pay her a decent salary. A woman who could take on such mundane chores as grocery shopping, cooking and cleaning, but also would be at home for Honor. But he wanted that woman to sit in the background of his life, not become a major part of it. To disappear into the wallpaper at night when he was home.

Walter's laughing response was that Chad's notions were more than a little out of date. In his experience, Walter said, such creatures existed only in the comics.

Now Chad sighed again, readily admitting he wasn't overly thrilled with giving up his bachelor's existence or having to share his apartment. He hadn't wanted to share that much of his life with any woman. A man who let a woman get the idea she was a staple in his life had to be ready for trouble, because she'd take over for sure. Look what had happened with his dad after he married Sandra.

Chad had barely seen his dad after that. Sandra had taken over his dad's life like a tornado, and then the couple hadn't had time for him. Even holidays had been sketchy of family togetherness.

That thought brought him back to his problem. The ideal woman for his and Honor's needs would have to take on a complex role. Obviously. What shocked him was that Spring seemed already to have fulfilled it. Honor certainly thought so.

His sister was mostly still an unknown quantity in *his* life, and he had yet to learn her habits, her thoughts, her ambitions for the future.

Chad rose and left the deli to stroll back to the office. His stack of work would take weeks to catch up, but he had to get his personal life on track before he could concentrate fully on anything else.

Most of his current dilemma was his own fault, he admitted with a discontented sigh. Selfishly, he'd put off really thinking of his sister's needs until after his stint in Europe. He'd allowed his own drive to take care of business to overrule his brotherly instinct.

However, the arrangement for his European corporate journey had already been in place when, only three weeks before he was to leave, his father died. No one else in the company could have taken his place without major upheaval. So he'd scrambled to take care of the necessary arrangements for the funeral and gain Honor a placement in a good boarding school.

Then Honor had shocked him with the announcement that she wanted to live with him, instead. He hadn't been ready for that, but he hadn't the heart to tell her she couldn't, since he was her closest living relative. She'd barely been installed in his home with Mrs. Hinkle before he left.

Now he had to step up to the plate of taking care of his family obligations. He owed his dad that loyalty, at least. Besides, his sister needed him.

And much to his dismay, he thought Honor Suzanne needed Spring. His sister seemed to have latched on to Spring as though the young woman were the sibling, instead of him. The affection and bonding between the two had already been set.

Spring had filled a very empty place in Honor's life, he supposed. A place he now readily admitted *he* hadn't been ready to fill. He'd be a real jerk to yank Honor out of that comfortable situation just when she had grown comfortable with it.

He'd have to face it, he thought as he let a sigh escape. Now he had two young women in residence—two young women with whom he had to learn to live.

He hadn't had a roommate since college.

He'd never had a female roommate at all.

He'd never felt responsible for another person's behavior, either, he discovered when he returned to his office. Now he felt it in spades.

Spring was there. To his surprise, he was met with a cluster of people standing around outside his office door, and found Spring in the middle.

Dressed in a long silky print skirt and ruffled blouse the color of her blue-green eyes, Spring seemed to be the center of attention from young Kevin Jensen from accounting and Stephan Appostalokas, the student intern from Greece. Stephan smiled down at her with all the subtleties of a strutting rooster, while Kevin brushed a hand through his long, stylishly cut hair. Chad had seen Kevin use the practiced gesture when charming all the young single women in the office.

Spring obviously enjoyed the attention. What young woman wouldn't? Chad reminded himself. She giggled at something Stephan said, and offered an inclusive, sparkling glance toward Kevin.

Chad felt like snarling. What on earth was she doing here? What did she want? Where was his assistant Anne?

Instead, he asked, "What's happening?" with all the aplomb he could muster.

He nodded at the two young men with a questioning glance, following which they speedily made their excuses and melted away. But not without backward glances, he noted.

Oh, fine! Now he'd have to fend off male curiosity over the young woman.

"Oh, there you are," Spring said brightly.

Her mouth curved, giving him the kind of welcome that he thought would please any prospective boyfriend. Didn't the girl have any common sense? Couldn't she smile less seductively? Less personally?

"—I brought down the folder you left on the coffee table last night. I was afraid you may need it."

So much for keeping his private and personal lives separate. By the look on Kevin's face, everyone in the office would now buzz with talk of his "live-in girlfriend." Would they even believe the truth if he explained? Not likely.

"Actually, I don't need it." He accepted the folder, but barely glanced at it. "However, I should have picked it up."

Living alone, he'd never have bothered.

"I did call to ask you about it, but your assistant said you'd gone to lunch."

"Of course." He cleared his throat. "Well, thanks."

His glance swept her, noticing how pretty she looked. Too soft for a briskly paced office. And she wore makeup today, a little mascara emphasizing her wide eyes.

She wasn't anything like his very efficient, conservatively dressed assistant, just returning after her own lunch hour. Like the capable professional she was, Anne hid her curiosity of his visitor under a well-trained facade.

Spring didn't hide hers toward the other woman at all. She smiled in a friendly manner, giving Anne her acknowledgment with a polite nod.

"Anne, this is my sister's friend, Spring Barbour." Chad felt forced to make introductions. If he didn't, the speculation would climb ever higher. "Anne Martin, my assistant."

"Hi," Spring greeted.

Anne returned the greeting.

"Is that all?" he asked Spring, barely refraining from a snap. This wasn't a party, after all.

"Yes, I'll be on my way." Her eyelashes fluttered. "I have an interview. But don't worry, I'll be home by the time Honor is. See you tonight."

"Sure." He watched her leave, making her way through the outer office toward the front reception area. At one point, she raised a hand and waved to someone. Kevin or Stephan?

Chad turned toward his office and caught Anne's speculative gaze, clearly amused in spite of herself, before she hastily averted it.

He kept his irritation from developing into a groan with a gritting of his teeth. He'd have to talk with Spring about office deportment.

Yet she didn't work in his office, and she hadn't really done anything wrong. His irritation at her wasn't appropriate. She'd only intended to do him a favor. He'd have to remember to thank her again.

But he didn't need any more of those kind of favors from Spring.

Chapter Seven

A few days later, Honor skidded to a stop on the polished foyer floor just as her brother came in a few moments before seven.

"Chad, can we go to a movie tonight?"

In the kitchen, Spring shoved a glass under the spigot on the refrigerator that gave out ice, and let it clink into the tumbler. The evening meal was almost ready.

"Tonight?" Chad's voice drifted around the corner. He sounded tired and distracted. "What about school tomorrow?"

"Aw, Chad. This is the last week of school," Honor replied, her tone persuasive. "There's not much going on tomorrow, we're just marking time. I won't miss much if I'm sleepy. And I haven't had a chance to see that movie."

"What's so important about it?"

"All the kids have seen it but me. It's really funny."

"I don't know, honey. I've got some work I have to wrap up." Spring heard his briefcase slide to the floor. "Besides, I have to fly out to Chicago tomorrow for a couple of days."

"Again?" Honor complained. "I thought you were through traveling for a while after you got home from Europe."

"Sorry. But that's why we have Spring with us, isn't it?"

"Then you won't care if Spring and I go, will you?"

"Um…"

Spring stepped from the kitchen, wearing a blue print summer dress with sandals. "I heard that, Honor," she said with a chuckle. "That movie is out of bounds, and you know it."

"Aw, shucks!" Honor said with a grimace. But then her mouth tilted into a grin as she said to Spring, "Thought you were chipping ice."

"Out of bounds?" Chad questioned, his brows raised, looking from one to the other. "Who says it's out of bounds?"

Chad loosened his tie and pulled it clear of his shirt. He hadn't a clue what this game was about, Spring thought. His mouth tightened as a frown puckered his brow. His look clearly said it was his choice as to what his sister could or could not do.

Actually, Spring agreed he should be the one to

make the decisions for his sister. But the movie in question really wasn't suitable for a youngster. He at least needed her opinion.

"I already told Honor not tonight for me on *any* movie," she told him, letting her own smile surface. "But especially not that one."

"Aw, Chad. You're my favorite brother. I've hardly seen you since...well, forever!" Honor flattered and complained with a pretty pout. "I'd hoped we could do something fun together."

Spring could barely hold her amusement in check at Honor's attempt to play the guilt card and charm her brother at the same time. She wondered if he'd give in or even catch on to his sister's ploy.

"What's wrong with the movie?" Chad asked Spring.

"*R* rated. Not one I'd recommend easily."

Chad slid Spring a glance of pleased surprise. Maybe she was overstepping herself, but then again, he needed all the help he could get in dealing with this kind of thing. "Oh, yeah?"

"All the other kids have already seen it," Honor complained. "Why shouldn't I?"

A glimmer entered Chad's eyes.

"Honor Suzanne, I recall using that same claim to wheedle Dad into letting me do something I wanted to do when I was your age. If Spring said no, I think we should accept that, don't you? What is this, anyway? You were quite happy to abide by her decisions all those weeks I was away."

"Dinner's on," Spring said, refraining from adding to what she thought of as Chad's first real lesson in parenting a teen. Better that she hold her tongue. If she could.

"Yeah, but you're home now," Honor said, wrapping her hands affectionately around his arm as they strolled into the kitchen. "Why couldn't you take me to the movie? I'm almost fifteen. You don't want me to be the only dorky kid in my class, do you, Chad? How can I learn to make good judgments if I'm never allowed to choose in the first place?"

"Spring already said no," he responded with a snap, giving way to tiredness. He pulled out a chair. "And as I mentioned, I have a meeting tomorrow that's absolutely pressing. What gives, anyway?"

"Don't be too hard on her, Chad." Spring bit her lip to keep her chuckle under control. Her resolve to stay out of this discussion hadn't lasted long enough to fill a New York minute.

Handing over a bottle of salad dressing, she let him see her amusement. "She's merely indulging in her constitutional right to behave like a teenager."

"How's that?"

"When one finds consent withheld from one parent or otherwise guardian, to seek consent for something one wants to do from the other adult. The one in her life most likely to give it."

Honor groaned a protest. "Spriiinng…"

"Oh." Chad looked blank a moment, then understanding dawned. Some of his exasperation fled. "She thought I'd be a softer touch."

"That's just about it," Spring agreed.

"I really do want to see that movie!"

"Sorry, sweetie," Spring said, her glance sympathetic. "I simply can't do a movie tonight. I have some sewing to finish and an application to fill out." She'd strolled around the famed garment district today and stepped inside a building with a well-known company name blazoned on the glass front door. It had taken all of her courage to ask for an employment application from the uninterested receptionist, but she'd triumphantly brought one home.

"Besides, there'll be lots of time next week after school's out for the summer when you'll positively be dying for things to do. And you start your summer ballet class soon."

"But not *that* movie." Chad spoke firmly. Without realizing it, he glanced at Spring for solid agreement. His gaze still carried a hint of harried frustration. He let a deep breath escape. "When I get back, we'll do something fun on the weekend. Okay?"

"Can we go to the beach?" Honor asked.

"Well, I had something different in mind," he said. "We'll save the beach for another time. There's plenty to do here in the city."

Honor's shoulders slumped. She tossed her brother a disgusted, doubtful look, then grumbled, "If you say so. If you don't have more absolutely pressing work to do."

Spring took a deep breath. The summer cooped up with an unfocused teen stretched out before them with all the appeal of an ice cream left in the hot July sun. Filling Honor's summer would be a challenge even in New York City. Chad needed a nudge to think about it, she guessed.

"I tell you what, Honor," she said. "As soon as school is out next week, we'll choose something special to do every day for a week. There're still a lot of spots around the city we haven't seen. And there're a bunch of old movies you'd love that we can rent." She named a few, then said, "How about a *Gone with the Wind* night?"

"What's *Gone with the Wind*?" Honor leaned on her elbow and played with her food.

Spring let her mouth drop. "You're from Virginia and have never heard of—?" She shot a glance toward Chad, who merely shrugged. "Well, we'll just have to fix that, won't we?"

Hours later, Spring left her bedroom to fetch a fresh ballpoint pen from the living room desk. Chad sat on the sofa, bare feet up on the table in front of him, his head back and his eyes closed. Loose papers spilled over his lap and onto the sofa. Beside his crossed feet on the coffee table, his laptop computer blinked an unread message.

She paused, loath to disturb him with her search. She could fill out that application tomorrow just as well as she could tonight, she decided. Still, she hesitated to simply leave him there. He needed to go to bed.

Chad had seemed unusually tired tonight, and after dinner and a quick shower, he'd gone right to the work he'd brought home. What was so pressing that he had to push it?

Had Honor been right when she'd mentioned that her brother was a workaholic? Or did he honestly love his work that much? Spring often lost herself in a creative project and couldn't stop until it was completed. Then again, perhaps he hid his emotions behind work.

What a waste! While she was ambitious for a career up to a point, there were too many other directions in life to enjoy, in Spring's opinion. Perhaps Chad needed some of that fun Honor insisted on pulling him into.

Would Chad agree? she wondered. A true workaholic found his fun in work, she'd been told. Would Chad go for some leisure activities?

She started forward, then stopped. Unable to help herself, she stood absolutely still to study his handsome features. For the first time, she admitted to herself how much simply looking at Chad gave her heart a kick. In normal circumstances, she might reveal how attractive she found him—but working for him put her in an awkward position. It wouldn't be wise.

She sometimes didn't know whether to continue to be Honor's friend or step back and give the two siblings time to close the gap between them. But Honor's loneliness was something on which she simply couldn't turn her back.

She'd skirted the subject of her employer when her sister Autumn asked her about him; she couldn't tell her sister that she'd stumbled for the first really handsome face she'd found since moving. Instead, she'd quizzed her sister on her budding romance with Brent and her latest art project.

Now she wished she had some of Autumn's artistic talent. She'd love to capture Chad on paper as he looked this very moment.

His hair reflected golden streaks under the lamplight, the same shadowed light that gave his nose strength while it softened the tired lines around his mouth. An unexpected tenderness crept over her; she wanted so badly to smooth those lines away, to feel the texture of his skin beneath her fingers.

The man *needed* to go to bed…to sleep solidly until morning. It couldn't hurt to merely suggest he call it a night.

Easing forward, she rounded the coffee table and gently lowered herself down beside him, keeping her focus squarely on his face. She leaned forward to place her hand on his shoulder. His soft breath brushed her skin, sending a quiver up her arm.

She sucked on her lower lip, moistening her mouth before she whispered, "Chad…Chad, it's late."

Slowly, his eyes blinked open. He didn't move

for a moment, his slumberous gaze fastening on her with a growing wakeful desire. Then his arm came around her, catching her in surprise, pulling her against his chest. His mouth settled on hers with drowsy need, sending a wild, sweet fluttering all through her body.

Instinct told her she teetered on a dangerous path. A path she might regret.

She didn't want to withdraw. She couldn't.

Then, Chad started to pull away, but didn't, quite. He blinked at her a moment. Then drowsiness was left behind as his mouth came down on hers again to take the kiss deeper.

She placed her hand against his cheek, her palm cradling his jaw, telling him with her own unspoken need just how much she liked his touch. Liked what was happening between them.

Then without warning, he let his arms drop and gently pushed her back. He rose in an awkward, guilty move, running a hand through his already disordered hair. Taking a long stride, he distanced himself. He didn't look at her.

Her breath still clogged her throat.

His sounded harsh. "I shouldn't have done that," he grated out as he abruptly paced away from her toward the windows.

Dealing with the sudden change, Spring brought her knees up to her chin, her arms tight around her legs, and watched him. She shivered with confusion. The imprint of his lips still lingered on hers.

"What a fool! I shouldn't—" He halted, staring out the windows at the never quite dark city, shoving his hands into denim pockets with an angry thrust. "You're in my employ! Taking advantage is unforgivable! I'm sorry, Spring. Lord help me…I don't know what got into me. You can…slap me silly, if you want. You have every right. I'm really…very sorry."

"I'm not," she murmured. She rose slowly and took a step toward him. "I don't want to slap you. I—"

She wanted the kiss to begin all over again. Dizzying, electrifying feelings of bliss ran a race with her thoughts.

"I suppose we should talk about this," he interrupted harshly, cutting off her jumbled response. "But not now, if you don't mind. It won't happen again, I promise you."

"But—"

He made a sudden lunge toward the tiny hall that led to his bedroom. "Tomorrow, please Spring," he muttered. "Let's talk about this when I'm…rational."

Chapter Eight

Spring spent a wakeful night with the feel of Chad's mouth still on her own. What should she do now? And furthermore, how should she respond to Chad's remark that their kiss should never have happened?

It hurt to think he was sorry to have kissed her.

Of course, it shouldn't have occurred! Not if Chad felt nothing for her, and had reacted only as a deprived male to the nearest eligible female. If he intended to remain her employer and she was here as Honor's companion, then he *should* be sorry.

They'd known each other for less than a month. They *both* should simply forget it ever happened.

Yet every tiny cell in her body recalled each second, each feeling of that kiss. Even now, she could recall how his hand had spread across her back to hold her closer.

She heartily hoped Chad's rest had carried just as many disturbing thoughts as hers. What right did the man have to kiss her like that, then say it didn't mean anything?

She was thankful that Chad was up and gone before her that morning.

Spring sighed more than once as she went about her day's chores, thinking of Chad and Honor. She longed to call Autumn, her nest mate. She and her twin had discussed every tidbit of their lives since before they could talk. But Autumn wasn't home.

Instead, Spring filled out her employment application and then one to a design school. Neither had her full attention. She went over them a third time as she tried to pull her mind into focus.

As she doodled on a stray envelope, her thoughts skipped back to Chad. Maybe by fall he'd find another housekeeper-cum-companion for his sister. Honor might not need her as much by then, having made her adjustments to living in the big city. Then Spring would have to find somewhere else to live. It might prove to be the best solution for both her and Chad.

It might prove to be the only solution. Otherwise...

How in the world were they to handle a long summer living together in the same apartment? With that awareness now between them? Bumping into each other at odd moments?

She'd just have to ignore him as best she could. That would do it. If he would stay out of her way.

But how did a woman resist the hunger? Natural hunger, most people would say, when all her hormones cried out to be fulfilled. When the movies and advertising and society and...just everyone, everywhere...said it was all right? Why couldn't she just give in to her feelings for Chad?

Josh Nolan, the teen minister, had come down hard on that particular temptation. He'd warned the teens that this would be one of their toughest fights as Christians—a daily choice to live Biblical principles over worldly ones.

Such choices seemed so hard, Spring mused, in their wide-open world. Especially when Chad tempted her with his very presence.

She let the pen drop from her hand. All the white space of the envelope carried little hearts, doodled in various sizes, entwined and marching along the sides. Spring smiled to herself. How childish they looked. Like something Honor would do, not a twenty-three-year-old woman of the world.

But she wasn't, quite. Although she wanted to be. With Chad.

Honor's trusting face floated up in her consciousness. The girl had to be considered. Spring couldn't disappoint her by becoming involved with Chad in that way.

Spring shoved the school application into a clean envelope. Although taking an intro design course was a prerequisite, perhaps the school would let her enter the advanced program if she could prove she already knew the basics. It couldn't hurt to ask, she supposed.

Pulling a sheet of fresh paper toward her, she penned the request quickly, before her resolve could fade. The sooner she left her current situation, the better off she'd be.

Leaning back in the desk chair, Spring's thoughts drifted to summer plans. Honor's school ended this week. The church needed more help with its Vacation Bible School, and there'd been talk of camp. She'd offer to help with the lunch crew during Bible School, while Honor attended the teen study. The teens were also committed to helping clean up a needy church across town during the afternoons. Dana, the minister's wife, had invited Spring to join them, and Spring wanted to do that.

Hanging out with Dana gave her a chance to really talk with an adult for a change, Spring thought. Someone besides a tall, lithe man who had only to look at her to make her feel like stumbling over her own two feet in excitement.

Getting up from the desk, she paced to the windows and looked out at the city.

She did miss her sister. But when she'd moved to New York, she and Autumn had agreed they were to find their own lives, their own identities, without clinging to each other so tightly.

Right now, her life was involved with keeping a

young girl happy and active. And too busy to dwell on her former life with her loving father. Enough to keep her out of trouble and out of her brother's hair, too, Spring supposed. With a tourist book in hand, the city attractions, and the local church activities, a summer in New York shouldn't be hard to take.

That would do it, Spring decided. She'd be so busy with Honor, she'd have no time for thinking about the way a certain pair of lips felt on hers. By fall, things would change. She'd have a better understanding of her own directions, as well as Honor's.

If Chad would simply stay out of her path.

The next evening, Spring and Honor were on the point of leaving the apartment, when Chad swung through the door.

"Where are you two off to?" he enquired, eyeing the Bible under Honor's arm as he picked up his messages. He barely glanced at Spring; the sight of her gave his heart too much of a knock.

He'd thought of her far too often for comfort while he took care of business in Chicago, setting off an irritation he couldn't rationalize. He didn't like anything to intrude on his concentration.

"It's a special Friday night teen rally at the church to kick off summer," Honor answered. "We're planning a camping trip for later down in the Pocono Mountains."

"Oh. Any supper left?" he asked. He thought he

did a good job of appearing uninterested. Yet he couldn't help noticing how Spring's hair, pulled back from her face, made her eyes appear wider. He'd told himself she couldn't possibly be as pretty as he'd thought her two nights ago. He'd reminded himself he'd been unusually vulnerable to a sweet and innocent young woman.

He still shouldn't have kissed her. He still wanted to do it again....

"There's some chicken salad," Spring told him, then offered hesitantly, "I could stay and make you a sandwich."

"No, don't do that. I'll manage on my own." He set his overnight bag on the floor and tossed the messages aside with only a glance. "What time will you be home?"

"About ten-thirty," Honor said.

"Is there something you need?" Spring asked, noting the flash of disappointment that he'd let cross his face. "Anything I missed in taking your messages?"

"No, I already had the messages by way of e-mail. I only thought we might take in a movie as Honor wanted to do earlier in the week," he said. For some reason, he'd looked forward to having the evening with his sister. And Spring. He could use an evening of relaxation with his family.

At least, that's what he told himself.

"Why don't you come along with us, instead?" Spring suggested, still with a note of hesitancy.

Enduring a teenage Bible study wasn't exactly first on his list of recreational excitements.

"Yeah, Chad," Honor begged before he could refuse. "Come with us. We can get something to eat afterward."

"Aren't we a little old for the event?" He pushed his suit coat back, his fingers hooking in his waist.

He tossed a teasing, half-cynical grin at Spring. She wore a denim skirt and a sleeveless plaid top, her hair tied back with half a dozen butterfly hair clips. At least she still *looked* a teenager.

That was the real problem. She was closer to Honor's age than to his own.

"Yeah, but there're often other adults there," Honor answered, winsome hope filling her brown eyes.

The girl still missed the closeness of attending church with their dad, Chad concluded. Her home church in Virginia had been a big part of her family life.

A shaft of envy shot up his back. What would he not have given to have his dad attend church and other functions with him and his mother? His father was never interested in those things.

He pushed the old resentment down; that was then and this was now. His father had changed when he'd married Sandra. Honor wasn't responsible for their father's choices.

"That's true. There're always a handful of adults that come to the teen activities. Dana never misses it," Spring offered. "She has a special affinity for youth. But the rally will be a little, uh…noisy with the kids."

"Noisy?" he said on a chuckle, appreciating her understatement. It wasn't hard for him to recall his own high school events.

Spring's eyes lit up in answer as a smile tugged at her mouth. "Um, yeah. Even so, I always get a lot out of the study that Josh Nolan gives. He's been teaching from Hebrews lately. A lot on faith."

Faith… Belief of God's involvement in man's personal life. Belief in the reality of Biblical truths, and a conscious decision to adhere to His tenants. Something Chad hadn't given much thought to in years.

Glancing from Honor to Spring, Chad felt a knot form in his jaw. He hadn't spent a Friday night in a church for years. Or a Sunday, either. Not since his mother had died. Shirley Alexander had been the parent involved in church, as he grew up. She'd been the parent who'd shared her faith with him, and the first person who taught him about God.

Douglas Alexander was uninterested in spiritual things, he'd often told young Chad, and refused to attend services with them. But he'd been a great father, nonetheless—until Chad's mom had died.

His dad had lost heart after that. He'd withdrawn from life for a long while, burying himself in his business and all but ignoring Chad during the boy's final high school years.

Chad learned to take care of himself. He'd chosen his college with only the help of his high school guidance counselor, and then taken himself there with little fanfare.

When his dad married Sandra, Chad had had little warning. Douglas proudly announced he'd met Sandra at a church singles event, and through Sandra, he'd found a strong commitment to the Lord. His life was changed, his dad declared; it was the best it had ever been.

Chad hadn't acknowledged his hurt. He'd even hidden his resentment of Sandra. Douglas hadn't been willing to please Chad's mother by attending church, and Chad recalled all too clearly his mother's deep sorrow over her husband's adamant refusal to talk of his spiritual needs.

After his dad's remarriage, Chad seldom visited the Virginia home, and when Honor was born within the year, he simply focused more closely on his own life.

For the past twelve years he'd functioned almost entirely alone. A single guy employed by a good law firm in New York, now a partner dedicated to his career, had little trouble finding friends among his associates. Especially women friends hoping to become a permanent part of his life. But he'd told all of them quite frankly that he didn't intend to marry until he reached forty, at least. He didn't want anyone to rearrange his life for him.

Now his life was rearranged, anyway. But Honor

was his sister; whether he liked it or not, she needed him to be her family.

He ran a hand through his hair, then down his jaw, feeling the day's growth. No time for a shave.

"Okay, why not. Let's go." He shoved his bag against the foyer wall. "Do we have a taxi waiting?"

"We always walk," Spring said.

Chad nodded, but pulled his phone out of his suit pocket and punched in the numbers for a cab.

"We could walk—it's not that far," Honor said, eager to leave.

"We could, but let's just have the taxi, okay?"

They took a cab for the short drive, arriving just as the assembly began to gather outside the huge stone church building.

"Hey." A pimple-faced boy spoke shyly to Honor as they walked around to the side entrance that Honor said would take them to the basement community room.

"How ya doing?" his taller companion added with a flashing, appreciative grin for Spring.

"Hi," Honor returned nonchalantly. Spring smiled, but said nothing.

Chad didn't miss the quick glances his way, silently asking who he was and assessing his presence. He felt like an invading outsider, and briefly wondered at his own sanity at consenting to come.

The huge room filled up fast, but no one hurried to sit. The kids were of mixed cultures, sizes, races, most of them well dressed while others obviously weren't. It didn't seem to matter.

"Oh, there's that girl, Leilani," Honor said, nodding toward a young girl standing against the far concrete wall. The youngster looked shyly out of great eyes darker than chocolate. "Dana says she's Hawaiian, and her name means something like 'wreath of heaven.'"

"She looks as though she could use someone to talk to," Spring suggested.

"Uh-huh. Okay." Honor was off like an arrow, tossing over her shoulder, "I'll find you two later."

Spring and Chad made their way to the folding chairs set in a great circle. As they sat down, Spring waved to a small blond woman about Chad's age. The woman held tightly to a toddler, who strained for freedom. They started toward Spring before being waylaid by a tall skinny youth.

Chad and Spring didn't talk. When she moved, he felt the brush of her knee; he shifted in his chair, shoving his hands in his pockets. Was this thing going to start on time? Sooner begun, sooner over.

A guitar began to strum, and a moment later the skinny youth sat down behind a set of drums, his knees folded almost to his chin.

Honor came back to them with Leilani in tow, and whispered introductions as praise music began to fill the big room to the ceiling and beyond. Everyone stood, and Chad followed their example. At least eighty kids took up the song and clapped in joyful rhythm, reminding him of a pep rally. Spring seemed at one with them, hardly older at all.

While Spring and Honor clapped, he let his hands rest at his side. He didn't feel a part of it.

Noisy, Spring had said? Yes, but it wasn't discordant or disordered. Rather, there was a jubilant reverence about the assembly.

The music changed to another lively tune, then finally a slower measured song with deeply worshipful meaning. Chad glanced at the overhead screen which splashed half-forgotten words of a song he'd once held precious, and began to sing, his voice rusty. As rusty as his faith.

When was the last time he'd really thought about God? he wondered. Or included Him in his life. Not for a long time—not even at his dad's funeral. He'd been too wrapped up in himself, in what had to be done, and what he was to do with Honor Suzanne.

He closed his eyes for a moment, letting go of the tight emotion he'd carried into the church with him. He hadn't even known he'd had it. On one side of him, he heard a sweet soprano, the voice expressing the words with loving attention. His sister. She certainly felt those words.

On his other side, Spring gave the music her low, pleasant alto without necessarily hitting every note.

Surprised, he glanced at her. Her lips moved with the words, yet he wasn't sure she could stay on tune. A smile tugged gently at his own mouth, and he almost stopped singing. Why the thought she couldn't carry a tune should delight him, he couldn't imagine. It was nothing to him. Was it?

When he glanced her way again, her eyes looked as deep as the sea and as soft as moss. She was singing off-key, and so appealing he wanted to laugh aloud.

Instead, he felt sudden gratitude for her presence grab him square in the chest. What in this wide world would he have done, what would have happened to Honor, if Spring hadn't come to them? She'd been an answer to a prayer when he hadn't even offered one up. In his ignorance, he'd stupidly left everything to a loose hit-and-miss plan.

He vowed to be a more thoughtful employer. To treat Spring with more respect. He didn't have to be a grouch all the time.

I must remember how young Spring still is, too. She has far more in common with this group, or those young men at my office, than with me.

But, oh! After that kiss, it wouldn't be an easy task.

Chapter Nine

"Leilani doesn't really like New York," Honor told Chad as he munched a double-decker sandwich.

Spring and Honor shared an order of spicy fries. Not very healthy, Spring had objected, but then she let it go when her mouth watered. "We should make some concessions to Honor's teen status, I suppose," she'd conceded, munching one with obvious enjoyment. "And I wouldn't want her to suffer these calories all alone."

Chad chuckled in spite of his serious mood, thinking her slender figure could take a lot of fries before showing an ounce of weight.

"New York does take some getting used to," Spring replied to Honor's remark. "And every city has its own personality, but especially this one."

"It's a vast change from Hawaii," Chad said.

"She's from the L.A. area, Chad," Honor informed her brother with a superior air. She picked up a long fry and studied it a moment before popping it into her mouth. "Spring, could we get her into the ballet class, do you think? She said she's had a couple of years of ballet and tap. Like me."

"I don't know, Honor," Spring replied. "I'm afraid the class has filled."

"Can we call tomorrow and see?"

"We?" Spring raised her brows. What was wrong with the youngster's mother making the call if that was what Leilani wanted?

"Um, will you do it?"

Spring sighed. Honor sometimes expected more from her than she had time for, and summer loomed ahead of them like a gaping hole waiting to be filled. "Sure, we can try."

"Great."

Chad followed the exchange with a slight frown. "All right, Honor, Spring has said she'd make the call to the ballet school, but that's all she's doing, understand? Your new friend will have to take it from there. It's not Spring's job to chase around town for your friends, and it's not fair for her to give up all her own free time to our causes. We're not paying her for twenty-four-seven."

Both Spring and Honor stared at Chad in surprise. Spring quickly dropped her lashes and picked at the last fry. He'd effectively reminded them she was in their home as an employee. She wasn't a family member.

Chad watched Spring's expression go very carefully blank and mentally kicked himself for speaking too bluntly. What was wrong with him lately?

Chad finished his soft drink, then placed his glass back on the table with precision. He clamped his teeth together to keep his thoughts from tumbling out. What did the women expect?

Did they think he never took notice of the running of his household? He'd given them every reason to think so for the last couple of months, he supposed. But on his flight home from Chicago, he'd given the matter quite a lot of thought. Spring had surfaced from those thoughts with every other breath. He found it downright irritating that she intruded so easily. He had to stop that, and stop it effectively. It could bring nothing but trouble, and he had too many things on his agenda to become sidetracked by a flirtation that had nowhere to go.

But he and Honor needed Spring. For now. And if he and Spring were to maintain a working relationship, he had to give them both some limits. Expecting too much of her, as they would a family member, was one of the limits he had to apply to himself.

It put an emotional safety net around them.

Without glancing Spring's way, he clamped his teeth around the last of his sandwich while his newly awakened conscious bit at his thoughts. He had to ignore the hurt he suspected Spring hid. And his natural instinct to console her. They both had to forget that kiss, or living together—in the same apartment, he amended quickly—would become impossible.

Perhaps by autumn, Honor wouldn't need a live-in companion. Honor would be fifteen in September. Surely, by then they could manage with only a housekeeping service to clean the apartment a couple of times a week.

"Okay." Unaware of either his or Spring's inner tensions, Honor accepted his dictate without argument. "But I want to invite Leilani over to hang out. That's okay, isn't it?"

"I suppose so, as long as you check with Spring first. If it doesn't put her out too much."

He risked a glance at Spring. She nodded, but didn't return his look.

"Okay—" he cleared his throat "—how about you and I taking off for the day up to Bear Mountain, and letting Spring have a day of freedom?"

"Really?" Honor squealed. Her brown eyes glowed like soft amber. "Oh, cool! But—" she turned to Spring "—what about our trip out to the Statue of Liberty?"

"That's not a problem." With a tentative smile for Chad, Spring insisted, "We can do that one day next week. Perhaps your friend would like to go, too."

Spring remained quiet on their stroll home, then gave a rather formal good-night as they all went to their rooms.

Much later, as Chad searched his desk for an address, he spotted a list Spring had made of American haute couture design companies headquartered in the city. The top three companies were checked off; apparently she'd already applied for work at her first choices. A second list was attached: Design Schools. Two had her check mark beside the name.

He pursed his mouth. She was serious enough about pursuing her goals. He felt satisfied; he could stop worrying and relax. Bide his time. Spring would be out of there to follow her career goals in another few months, leaving Honor and him to get on with their lives.

For Spring, Saturday felt like a long day. She had called Dana to meet her for lunch, but Dana couldn't make it. Still, Spring enjoyed her day of freedom.

She spent time searching out a fabric store she hadn't visited before, bought a nice piece of summer cotton, and gave momentary thought to the Help Wanted sign she spied by the cash register before deciding it would never work. She had lunch at a quiet restaurant and watched the other diners as she ate, observing their dress and body language, guessing at which ones were tourists. Then on her way home, she stopped at a video store and rented *Gone with the Wind* in anticipation of sharing the movie with Honor.

But Honor and Chad didn't return home until

nearly nine, so she entertained herself during the evening with a call to her sister.

"I tried to reach you earlier today," Autumn said, her tone eager.

"I was out shopping. Why didn't you leave a message?"

"Because what I wanted to tell you is too important. I had to tell you in person. Brent and I are getting married!"

"Well, that's no shock." Spring leapt up, letting excitement and sheer happiness for her sister send her into a dance step. "I knew the two of you were attracted to each other from that very first day. I thought it was only a matter of time."

"All right, smart mouth. So I knew you knew."

Spring broke into a chuckle, knowing her smile reflected its almost perfect match in Kansas City. "So when?"

"Next month," Autumn replied, her voice reflecting her shy streak. "We decided we didn't want to wait on a long engagement."

"Shoulda known. Well, you tell my new almost brother-in-law, he's a lucky man. No—more than lucky, he's a blessed man. And give him a hug from me. And little Timmy."

"I'll do that. Sis, I'll need something special to wear…"

"Of course." She pushed her hair away from her face and grabbed her sketch pad from beside her bed, flipping quickly to something she'd worked on just two days before. ''And I have a design that would look beautiful as a wedding dress, Autumn. I was thinking of you when I designed it. Shall I send you a sketch?''

Autumn laughed, the joyful bubbling laugh that Spring so missed. She and her sister had never lived apart until she'd come to New York. Yet their thoughts often took the same path at the same time, as though no distance separated them.

''No, surprise me. I know it'll be beautiful if you make it. And you will come home to be my maid of honor, won't you?''

''Dumb question. I'll make reservations on Monday. And I'll have to bring the dresses with me. Won't have time to ship them.''

''That's fine. It isn't as though we have to worry about fit.''

Over an hour later, after each detail of the wedding and Spring's trip home had been discussed at least three times, Spring finally hung up the phone. She immediately began her to-do and to-buy lists. It would take all her extra time for the next three weeks to make the wedding finery, but she couldn't have felt more joyful.

Getting a long weekend off from her position here wouldn't be a problem, Spring thought, not with Chad's new approach to her employment. She'd accumulated several days off. However, perhaps she'd ask to take Honor with her when she flew to Kansas City. They'd have a fine time.

After her sister's call, Spring had a hard time settling down with the book she'd been reading. She heartily wished she had a local friend with whom she could share her excitement.

It felt lonely in the apartment without Honor and Chad. She hadn't made many friends in New York, she realized. Time to spread her wings, she supposed. Join the singles group at church. If she was going to make a success of this transition in her life, then she had to meet a larger circle of people.

That's what she'd do, she promised herself. Just as soon as she had Autumn's wedding completed. After all, she didn't need to be on-call for Honor anymore.

However, that resolve didn't keep her heart from leaping with eagerness when she heard the key turn in the lock. She lowered her book, and looked over her shoulder as Chad and Honor came into the living room.

"Hi, you two. Did you have a nice day?"

"The best!" Honor plumped herself down on the couch beside Spring and chattered about her day.

"A good day," Chad agreed.

Chad paused, glancing at Spring as he slipped his keys into his pocket. The quick, searching look sent a shaft of yearning to her heart.

He quickly averted his attention to the blinking light on the answering machine and went to play the messages.

One was a business message, but one was an in

vitation from a woman named Melissa for dinner next week. Before meeting Chad, Spring hadn't been curious about his social life; now she wondered if Melissa was one of his regular girlfriends. Had she been one of the callers during those first weeks Spring had come to live with Honor? Spring couldn't honestly recall, and it didn't matter to her if Melissa was.

That's what Spring told herself.

Chad didn't enlighten her, merely saying good-night and that he would return his messages from his room.

Spring hid her curiosity and listened to Honor's recounting of her day. It took her a moment to be able to do more than make senseless noises of interest, but thankfully, Honor didn't notice.

When Honor winded down, she told the girl her own news. "I'll need a long weekend off by the end of the month. But you can come with me, if you like. If Chad doesn't object."

"Really? That's a super idea. I love weddings. And it's just before church camp."

Camp. Honor would be away for a whole week next month. That was good. Spring would have more time to recover after a hectic schedule of designing and sewing the wedding clothes. Her trip home wouldn't be a relaxing one.

Oh-oh... Not so good, Spring thought. She and Chad would continue to share the apartment. Alone. Together.

Her gaze flew to the hall doorway as though Chad would suddenly make an appearance to sweep her up into his arms.

The understanding of sweet temptation hit her hard. An old song of that title had been in Uncle William's record collection, a leftover of his youth. She and Autumn had played it once, and now, from the recesses of her memory, she recalled the pulsing music.

She swallowed hard, yanking her gaze back to Honor's enthusiastic chatter. Rain began to spatter against the window, and she thoroughly wished they had a balcony. She needed to cool down.

Definitely, she needed to gain control of her thoughts.

On Sunday, Spring dressed for church at the usual time. Outside, clouds obscured the sun. Since she hadn't spoken to Honor or Chad about their Sunday plans, she didn't know what they intended to do with their day, but the rainy weather didn't invite outdoor activity.

For once, Honor was in the kitchen before her, popping whole wheat bread into the toaster. Spring made coffee and poured juice.

"Can we leave a little early this morning, Spring?" the girl asked, giving her the clue that their usual plans to attend church together hadn't been disturbed. "I want to talk to Josh and Mrs. Barron about signing up for the camp. They're almost filled up, and I don't want to lose out."

"Sure, I don't see why not."

"Then let's hurry."

"Calm down, Honor," Chad said, strolling into the kitchen. He was dressed except for a tie and jacket. "I want some coffee first. We'll grab a taxi like we did the other night."

"Okay. I'll call." Honor grabbed her buttered toast and dashed out of the kitchen.

Chad poured his cup of coffee and sat down at the table. Spring busied herself with moving things around on the counter, not looking at him. He'd meant it. He planned to take Honor to church.

"Would you like some cereal?" she asked, wondering if she was expected to be one of their group or if she was on her own for the day.

He glanced at her sleeveless dress in soft turquoise, his gaze taking in her slender figure before lifting to her face for a fleeting moment. But it didn't linger, skittering toward the toast in her hand.

"No. A piece of toast will do for now. Let's have brunch after church, if you don't mind."

"That sounds nice."

She set a carton of milk in front of him, just as he reached for the butter. His hand brushed her arm, the back of his knuckles warm on her skin. She pressed her lips together and stepped away without uttering a sound. She ignored the tiny quiver it sent rushing up her arm.

They wouldn't become involved...they wouldn't. They had agreed. She'd get over this...this *thing* that came over her every time he came into the room.

Spring left the kitchen to fetch her matching jacket, which was laying across her bed with her purse and Bible. She spent what felt like a long five minutes on a lipstick touch-up before she met the other two in the living room.

The Sunday morning city streets were almost quiet in the rain. They rode the few blocks to the church in silence, with Honor sitting between Chad and Spring. Chad produced an umbrella to shield them for the few yards between the taxi and the church doors.

For the few months they'd been attending the church, Spring and Honor always sat on the far left of the church auditorium, where the teens and college kids gathered. Honor headed that way when they arrived, but Chad changed directions and guided them to seating across the aisle.

Honor insisted on sitting in the aisle seat so she could at least wave to the kids opposite. It left Chad sitting next to Spring again. Within moments she found herself squeezed closer against him, as a young family crowded into the pew on her other side.

His shoulder brushed hers; his long fingers touched hers while they shared a songbook; she caught the musky fragrance of his aftershave. It was heady stuff.

The service moved along its usual pattern. Spring struggled to close her thoughts to all but the prayers, the music, the sermon, the reading of the Word. She drew in a deep breath. She needed the spiritual closeness of the One whom they worshiped.

This morning Senior Pastor was reading from John. "*'I am the bread of life... I am the gate... I am the good shepherd... I am the light of the world....'*"

Jesus's own words of who he was and his life's purpose. And they remained today as alive as yesterday. Scriptures requiring steps of faith, giving directions for salvation.

They had already taken root in her heart.

"*...if you love me, you will obey what I command.*"

Beside her, Spring felt Chad turn, knew his gaze rested on her. Turning slightly, she felt caught in a great wave of awareness of him, of his masculinity.

Lord, she prayed frantically. *If you love me you'll give me some of your strength to withstand all this temptation.*

That word instantly recalled Honor's funny interpretation of losing her patience with a librarian—her idea of temptation. It gave Spring a mental shake, a mild chuckle. Temptation did, sure enough, come in all sizes and packages.

Because pure, unadulterated temptation to fall into Chad's inviting gaze, into his eager arms, was likely to consume her if they were left alone for long. What in the world was she to do during that week while Honor was away at camp?

Chapter Ten

Honor started her ballet class on Tuesday. The class had been filled, so her friend Leilani had been placed on a waiting list. Honor promised to privately teach her everything she learned in class, so her friend wouldn't miss anything. The girls made plans for Leilani to come to the apartment in the afternoon.

While Honor attended the class, Spring rushed downtown to the fabric story she'd just visited on Saturday. Choosing with care, she splurged on the most exquisite lace she could find for the wedding gown bodice she would make for Autumn. She matched that with a creamy satin, and then chose a rose-colored fabric of graduating shades for her own dress.

She could hardly wait to cut into the fabric. She'd need the expansive dining room table to lay it all out. To properly sew it, too, without wrinkling it unduly.

Would Chad object? She hadn't exactly explained all that was involved in her sewing needs.

On Sunday, he'd given her permission to take an extended weekend for her sister's wedding. He'd also mentioned he had a heavy workweek coming up, with long days ahead. They shouldn't expect him on time for dinner unless they heard from him. He'd be home only to sleep.

If she was careful always to pick up all her materials, surely he wouldn't object to her use of the dining room. He'd hardly notice, really.

And while she lay out the bodice this evening, she'd pop the *Gone with the Wind* tape into the VCR for Honor. It was due for return tomorrow. Spring hoped it might spark an interest in the girl for American history, a subject Honor rolled her eyes over and had passed by the skin of her teeth. But would the child dislike it so much if she watched a film that told of the Civil War era and someone of her own age with whom to watch it? If it didn't feel like homework?

She arrived back at the ballet school just as the intermediate class was dissolving into the advanced session. Honor was dressed, ready to go.

"I rented a special movie for you to watch," said Spring.

"What is it?"

"Something fun. What time is Leilani coming?"

"Right after lunch."

"Great."

Spring kept Honor guessing about the movie during lunch. She wanted it to be a pleasant surprise. When Leilani arrived, the girls disappeared into Honor's room for half an hour before they emerged in shorts and their practice shoes. They shoved one of the chairs up against the sofa, put on the CD Honor had chosen and began to practice.

Spring laid out the lace fabric and studied its pattern to decide which direction she wanted to cut it. She took extra time to lay out her pattern pieces; none of them matched a commercial pattern. Each had been one she'd brought with her from home, measured and made long ago to fit both her and her twin's body to perfection. There was very little difference between them; Autumn was taller by half an inch, but a smidgen smaller in the bust. Spring needed only to make minor changes in the standard form to achieve the look she wanted.

Spring didn't hear the front door open. She wasn't aware Chad had strolled in, observing them all a moment before he was discovered. The girls, using straight-backed dining chairs in place of a practice bar, had gone through their ballet paces, and now Leilani was demonstrating some of her native dance techniques. They noticed Chad only when they stopped to giggle.

"Oh!" Spring looked up, her hand flying to remove the silk straight pins in her mouth. "Chad.

What are you doing home in the middle of the afternoon? Is anything wrong?''

"No. Had to pick up my car. I need to run up to Connecticut for the rest of the day. Sorry. Meant to mention it this morning.''

"Guess that means you'll be late getting home,'' Spring said.

"Can Leilani sleep over?'' Honor asked.

Chad looked at Spring. "Is that okay with you?''

"It's fine with me,'' she answered. "If her mother approves.''

"Great. Can we get Chinese take-out?'' Honor begged.

Chad again glanced at Spring, his gaze lingering a moment. "Sure. Why not?''

Spring smoothed her hair behind her shoulder. She'd given it a long brushing last night, after she'd noticed how Chad's gaze frequently followed her habitual movement.

Breaking eye contact, he turned abruptly and headed purposely toward his desk.

"Cool!'' Honor began. "Can we go—?''

"No, stay in tonight, Honor.'' He sat his briefcase down, clicking it open. He pulled a folder out of the stack on his desk and placed it in the briefcase. "Spring has more to do than let you run every night.''

"But it's summer, Chad.''

"I tell you what—hang in here at home this week

while I put in my time at work, and we'll go skating on Sunday after church.''

"Really? Where? I didn't bring my skates, I left them in Virginia.''

"Never mind that. We'll get some new ones. Inlines. We'll join the street skating in Central Park. It's like a big party.''

"Can Leilani go?''

"Sure. We'll all go.''

He left shortly after that, barely saying goodbye, as though his mind centered on business. Spring sighed with relief. He didn't seem to care that she was making use of the dining room table for her sewing project.

The girls put in a new CD and threw themselves down on the couch to begin a discussion of who's who in the world of the church circle teenagers. Spring listened, trying to recall faces to match the names she heard mentioned, waiting to hear if any specific boy's name surfaced more than once or twice.

Several did. Spring turned away to hide her smile. It hadn't been that long ago since she'd been just as eager to talk about boys. The closest she'd come to a steady boyfriend had been Tyler Goth, but they'd been friends more than anything else.

Then again, it hadn't been that long since she'd filled her sister's ears about Chad.

She sighed and turned her attention back to the lace. She hadn't had that much to say about him lately. What could she tell Autumn, beyond the fact that she found him attractive, but he had other interests?

By the time Chad returned home, Spring and the girls were sprawled out in front of the TV, their gazes glued to the screen. From the music and well-remembered dialogue, he could tell the movie was ending.

"Hello, ladies," he said in greeting.

No one answered. No one looked his way.

He tried again. "Uh...hello?"

"Shush!" Honor responded with a hiss.

Her gaze still on the TV, Spring held up her hand as the credits began to roll. Chad heard three collective sighs.

Chad chuckled. "Well, I don't have to guess at how you three spent your evening. I'm sorry I missed it."

"Whew!" Honor sank into the couch, finally looking his way. "We watched the *whole* movie."

"Did you enjoy it?"

"Actually, we did. I'd love to try on one of those ball gowns. Or the dress Scarlett wore for that barbecue scene."

"I liked that blood-red dress she wore toward the end of the movie," Leilani said, dreamy-eyed. "But I wouldn't like it all the time."

"Yeah, it woulda been hard to move around in all those petticoats," Honor said, sounding in a reflective mood. "With no air-conditioning, yet. But the movie was sad, wasn't it? All that fighting and destruction. Now I know why Daddy took me to see those old battlefields. He told me we had an ancestor on each side. One blue and one gray."

"That's right. Dad had a fascination for American history, but especially the Civil War. He had real pride in both sides of his family."

Honor said, "Hey, Chad. Spring says the next time we go North a ways, we ought to tour West Point. Talk about the Revolutionary War and times, too. Benedict Arnold and all that. Can we do that soon?"

"Sure, sometime. I haven't been there in years."

He glanced at Spring as she turned away, picking up the empty popcorn bowl. Leilani sat down in the corner of the couch. She seemed content to simply observe them, her chocolate eyes dark but lively.

Chad stuck his hands in his pockets and drew out his change and keys, tossing them on the desk next to his briefcase. A couple of messages lay against his phone. He picked them up but didn't read them, thinking of a brief he needed to check through before an early morning meeting. He didn't want to get into it now. It could wait.

Spring stopped the movie and ejected the tape. "I bet we can find an old film or two that would make that period of history interesting. And novels."

He recalled a few of his own trips to historical sites with his dad. Before his mother died, he'd known Washington, D.C., its museums, monuments and surrounding sites, very well. East of there, Annapolis had been one of his favorite jaunts. He'd loved visiting the Naval Academy, though he had no desire to attend as a student.

Thinking about his father's passion for American history, he frowned. "Say, Honor. What did Dad do with his collection of old letters, do you know?"

Chad hadn't thought of his father's collection in a long time. He used to know just how many famous signatures it contained. Twenty-seven, twenty-eight?

"Uh-uh. I forgot all about 'em," Honor answered. "Probably still put away in his study someplace. Or his safe. I don't think he sold them."

Chad nodded. After the funeral, he'd briefly checked the safe, but couldn't recall seeing the letters. He'd hired an estate agent to close up the house and look after it. The property came with a few acres not far from Washington's home, Mt. Vernon.

They had to make a few decisions about the house and its contents soon, he supposed. But he wasn't sure his sister could easily let it go. Until a few months ago, it was the only home she'd known.

His thought was diverted as Spring collected a few sewing items, lace pieces that she laid carefully in a large basket. She then set the whole basket down on the floor beside the club chair. A small package of what looked like pearls dropped from the chair arm. She whisked the package into the basket with a flick of her wrist. She glanced his way, as if wondering whether he'd noticed.

He noticed. Without appearing to pay much attention, he noticed. Always, in spite of himself, he took in her graceful way of moving, the way her hair swung, or the curves of her profile.

He switched his attention back to his sister.

"We should run down to Virginia sometime this summer, too," he said slowly, trying to read his sister's face. "Stay at the old house a few days. Would you like that?"

"Sure." But Honor's lashes flickered when she spoke, and she averted her eyes too quickly. Only the tense line of her mouth let him know how painful she found the prospect. She wasn't ready.

He looked toward Spring, feeling helpless. What could he do? She bit her lip and flashed him an empathetic glance, then changed the subject.

"Would anyone like more popcorn?"

"Uh-huh. I'll make it." Honor hopped up and spun out to the kitchen. "Anyone for Parmesan cheese on it?"

"Sounds good." Spring curled up in the club chair and turned to their young guest. "Leilani, maybe you'd tell us more of your Hawaiian history."

"Um, what do you want to know? I've never lived there."

"Oh. Well, we can still have fun with a study on it. Hey, why don't we do an island theme evening and do some foods and decorations from there? We can go to the library and find out about the last Hawaiian royalty. Maybe your mom would be willing to help. Shall I ask her?''

Honor came in with more popcorn and napkins. She put them on the coffee table and sank onto the couch next to her friend. ''Super. Can we?''

''Okay.'' Leilani's eyes lit up with pleasure. She took a napkin and unfolded it carefully in her lap. ''That would be nice. Mom loves making new friends, and we haven't been in New York long.''

''I'll do an Internet search on the islands,'' Chad offered. He didn't own a desktop computer, and depended only on his laptop for home use. Perhaps it was time to purchase one for his sister; he hadn't thought of it before. ''These days we can get everything on the Internet. Even history.''

He coiled himself down to sit on the floor near the popcorn bowl, across from Spring. Once again he noticed the basket sitting half-hidden beside her chair, a corner of lace fabric hanging over its edge. What was she making? Something else to show off her designs?

Spring kicked off her shoes and tucked her feet up under her. She had slender ankles and straight little toes, the nails painted a pale pink.

Grabbing a handful of popcorn, he munched as he pulled out the two messages he'd tucked into his shirt pocket. Both were from his assistant, Anne. His early morning appointment would be delayed by thirty minutes. And he'd been asked to dinner at Jonathan Feathers's home; he should bring a dinner partner.

He supposed he'd ask Melissa. They'd dated a few times in the most casual way just before he'd gone to Europe; he hadn't called her since returning home.

Or should he take Anne? Anne might be a better choice. Anne was eager to move up in the company, and she'd be grateful for the invitation. She'd be professional and wouldn't expect anything personal from him.

Across from him, Spring joined the two girls in another giggle. He'd missed the joke.

But he didn't miss how close she seemed in age to the fourteen-year-olds.

Yes… Anne would be the best choice. He didn't feel a particle of romantic interest in Anne.

Chapter Eleven

Without school as her focus, Honor grew easily bored, complaining there was little to do alone in a high-rise apartment. The big city had curtailed the freedom she'd known in her childhood home, she complained. But at not-quite fifteen, Chad wasn't about to let her go far without a companion.

That dictate curtailed Spring's freedom, as well.

Spring tried assigning Honor to reading projects with only moderate success. They took long walks for exercise, took the promised trip to the Statue of Liberty, and visited other city sites. Leilani came along at times, but since she had to help her mother with her younger siblings, she couldn't always go.

Spring, both patient and impatient, tried to balance the days with humor. But the wedding dress was in slow progress. A good deal of the sewing had to be done in stolen bits of time.

Spring did manage to hand-sew clusters of tiny pearls along the wide lace neckline during their evening hours of TV watching. She was aware of Chad's gaze more than once, his attention straying her way from a magazine or one of his legal briefs.

One morning when Leilani visited, she'd given the girls a lesson on how to lay out a pattern when she cut the rose satin for her own maid of honor dress. They appeared intrigued and eager to see it complete, but not interested enough to get into a sewing project for themselves.

Spring racked her brain for additional activities to fill the summer. The dance class held Honor's excitement well enough, as did the church teen Bible studies. Camp lay ahead like a carrot stick. The girls mentioned it only a dozen times a day.

Chad said nothing about her sewing, for which she was thankful. He came home most evenings by seven, often helping to clear away supper dishes. Then he would usually spend an hour or so at his desk catching up on work.

Yet, when the teen Bible study came round again, he changed into casual clothes and accompanied them. This time, Dana sat next to him, making him welcome before Josh began the evening.

And true to his promise, on Sunday after church, he pulled out and handed both Honor and Spring big square boxes. Inside each were identical pairs of skates, with knee and elbow pads crammed in the corners.

"Oh, Chad. You're the best brother in the whole world!" Honor exclaimed. She stretched to kiss his cheek, catching him by surprise. "Thanks. These are great! I'm going to call Leilani."

His eyes softening, he turned to Spring.

"Me?" Spring dropped her mouth, staring at him uncertainly as he offered her the skate box. She rose slowly from the window chair where she'd been threading a needle. "You bought me skates, too?"

"Said we'd all go, didn't I?" He didn't give a more complete explanation of why he'd included Spring in the proposed outing. He'd already dug into his closet for his skates and had changed into long shorts and a dark blue sweatshirt that had its arms and neck cut away. "It's a nice day to be outside, it's good exercise, it's summertime, and we all need the break. Enough reasons. You didn't plan to do anything else today, did you?"

"I had thought to finish the hem in the wedding dress," she said, her gaze roaming to her handwork basket, which seldom left its place these days beside the chair.

"Not this afternoon." He leaned against the door frame, watching her examine the skates. "Technically, you should have the whole day out of this apartment and off to yourself. But this will be something you'll enjoy, I promise you."

"Are you sure these are the right size?"

"You wear a seven shoe, don't you?"

"Yes, but how did you know?"

"That was easy," he said, his tone dropping a notch, slowing. Evoking a response that tickled along her limbs. "I picked up one of yours and looked."

"Easy..." That would be true enough, Spring mused, almost getting lost in his gaze once again. She had a bad habit of kicking off her shoes whenever she could. The thought that he'd handled one sent a shock wave of intimacy racing down to her fingertips.

Why had he included her in his gift giving? Did he *intend* to lump her together with his sister?

Spring drew a confused breath. The gift didn't feel like a casual one. But Chad didn't intend for it to mean anything personal, either. "Thanks for thinking of me..."

Honor raced back into the living room, breezily reporting her friend's reaction to their plan as "cool."

"Hurry along to change," Chad instructed. He straightened, as though eager to leave. "Did you tell Leilani where to find us?"

"Uh-huh," Honor said as she dashed again toward her room. "She's bringing her two brothers."

So, Spring mused, staring after her, Chad and Honor had discussed their afternoon plans already.

"You don't want to skate in that skirt, do you?" His gaze had switched back to her.

"No, of course not, but—" Spring tried to think of a graceful refusal, but after gazing at the shiny new skates, not a single excuse seemed adequate. That she couldn't skate well wouldn't matter; she could learn.

"Okay, let's scoot. I promised to meet friends later."

Spring felt moved along as though she were a leaf in a stream at flood stage. In her room, she pulled on jeans and a pink T-shirt, and grabbed a pair of thick socks.

In Central Park, the skaters were already out in numbers. Chad and the three women found a spot to sit on the grass near a tree where they changed into their skates. Chad put their shoes into the backpack he'd brought for that purpose, then slipped it onto his shoulders.

Spring dawdled. The skates felt heavy. It had been years since she had skated, and she'd never used in-lines before.

Honor was a whiz. She zoomed away like a rocket, bird flying, while Spring gazed after her in wonder. Next to her, Chad stood up and took to the street, where he did a quick, tight circle.

Honor came sailing back, calling for her to hurry up. Spring gave a great sigh. Obviously, both the Alexanders were gifted and proficient.

She bent her head and pretended the laces in her left skate needed rethreading. Chad took a spin halfway up the block before returning to her.

A long line of skaters danced by, holding hands like a string of paper dolls of varied races, mixed heights and builds, adults and youngsters alike. They were as individually dressed as though of God's own rainbow design.

Spring remained sitting on the edge of the walk. A tiny boy bumped into her, his skates hitting her thigh. She glanced up at his mother and apologized.

She couldn't remain here, she decided. Glancing around, she saw that Honor had joined a circle of skaters beginning a new line connection. Leilani skated up to Honor. The girl was accompanied by an older boy; they looked so much alike that Spring guessed he was her brother. They joined the circle, opening and closing it like a pulsing star.

Where was Chad? She hadn't seen him for a few moments. Now was her chance, she guessed, before he came back to see how clumsy she was on skates.

Grasping the tree, she wobbly got to her feet. How did one stand on these single-line rollers?

She shoved off on stiff legs and made it to a bench. She grabbed the back, shaking the gray-haired elderly lady who'd had the bravery to pause there, chattering on her mobile phone.

"Sorry, ma'am."

She couldn't quite bring herself to let go entirely. The woman gave her an affronted stare. She licked her lips. "Um, sorry."

She took a tentative glide, sailing a few feet before stopping herself on the grass, waving wildly to regain her balance. She paused long enough to let her heart slow down.

Where had Chad and Honor gone? Searching the crowd, she spotted Honor still with her friends. Satisfied, Spring felt content to watch them.

Chad seemed to have vanished.

"Spring?" She heard a masculine voice. Not Chad's.

Turning, fighting to remain upright, she searched the crowd for a face she recognized. Kevin Jensen from Chad's office emerged from a clutch of sidelined observers.

Kevin smiled, giving her a delighted welcome. "Hi."

"Oh, hello. Are you here to skate?"

"Just got here," he said with a pleased nod. "Are you here alone?"

"Not exactly. Chad and Honor are in this crowd somewhere," she said, searching the skaters around her. "I've lost them for the moment."

"They're probably hooked up already. Don't worry, you can stick with me and Stephan. Sooner or later everyone skates by." Kevin turned to call over his shoulder. "Hey, Stephan, look who I've found."

Stephan Appostalokas, already on skates, broke away from the group with which he'd been talking. "Hello, Spring. You have come to join us, yes?"

He gave her a slow smile, and his dark eyes sparkled flirtatiously. Spring suspected he responded to all women the same way, but she couldn't help herself. She smiled in return.

"Well, I'm really not very experienced," she murmured, brushing her hair from her eyes. "I'm afraid I'll hold you back."

"Oh, you couldn't hold Stephan back," Kevin tossed out. "He'd simply skate 'round you in circles. But I'm still gaining my balance. Here...wait till I get my blades on and we can hold on to each other."

The gray-haired lady got up and left, so Spring took a deep breath and wobbled toward the bench. She sank onto it gratefully. Stephan left them to skate in and out of a passing line, enticed by a young blond woman in red shorts.

Kevin sat beside her, shucked his loafers and pulled on well-worn skates. She doubted he was quite the novice at this that he pretended to be.

Honor and her friend skidded to a stop in front of her. Even Leilani appeared steady on her feet. Spring hid a sigh.

"Are you ready yet, Spring?" Honor asked.

"Um, not quite. This is Kevin. He works with your brother's firm."

Honor said hello, but seemed only mildly impressed with Spring's new friend. She focused on Spring. "Well, are you coming?"

"I'll be along, I guess." If she could. "You girls stick together, okay?"

The girls nodded and took off. Spring rose and tried a calculated glide. She felt steadier, but there was no way she'd ever keep up with the others. Her arms outspread for balance, she took another stride.

Keep up? She wasn't sure she could even turn back to the bench.

From behind her, she felt a hand on her shoulder and one against her waist, giving her stability. She tipped her chin, glancing over her shoulder expecting to see Kevin.

Instead, her glance tangled with Chad's. A flicker of possessiveness darkened his eyes for half an instant. Then he stepped forward, letting his hand slide down to her elbow, effectively embracing her in the traditional skater's position.

"I won't let you fall," he said in a low voice.

She sucked in a breath. Had he been behind her long? Obviously long enough to know she was floundering.

"Chad," Kevin greeted, coming up on her other side. His tone held a skeptical edge as he said, "Didn't know you still indulged in street skating."

"Kevin," Chad returned pleasantly enough. "Yeah, sure. Why not? I like the sport as well as most."

The two men stared at each other as though silently squaring off over disputed territory.

"Spring thought we'd lost you," Kevin said.

"Not even a little. I was just over by that tree, talking to someone."

Letting his arm drop from around her waist, Chad took her elbow. "Let's catch the girls."

"Not too fast, please?"

"No faster than you can manage."

"Here, I'll be your other bookend," Kevin said, defying the flash in Chad's eyes. He gave an irrepressible grin and took her other hand, threading it through his arm.

Stephan came swirling out of nowhere, twirling to skate backward while facing them. "What's up, eh? A party?"

"No, not a party," Chad said mildly. "Just a family outing."

"Oh. Too bad. But Spring would make any gathering a party."

Chad glided forward, propelling her along.

Feeling perfectly steady between the two men now, Spring laughed. "You are so bad, Stephan. Do you think women actually fall for that outrageous nonsense?"

"But, of course..." Stephan replied, grinning.

He didn't underestimate his own charm, Spring thought. But he was so ingenious about it, she only found him amusing.

"From Stephan, women buy into it all the time," Kevin said with a mock morose expression. "Why do you think I hang out with him? When they get tired of hanging on to his every flattery like a bunch of grapes on the vine, then some of them turn my way."

"But in Spring's case, it isn't flattery," Stephan insisted. "Why don't we make a party? We can all meet at that little spaghetti place just across town.

You know the one, Chad. I saw you there once with that blonde with the long legs.''

Chad tightened his mouth. ''Can't tonight, Stephan. We promised to meet family friends later.''

Who? What friends? He hadn't mentioned the date to her, nor to Honor, she thought. Spring turned to question him, but Chad wouldn't meet her eye.

''Well, that doesn't include—'' she started.

''The Peebles asked us to meet them for a bite. They are especially looking forward to seeing you again, Spring. Seems you and Honor are favorites with their children.''

''Oh.'' She was fond of the Peebles, but puzzled over why Chad hadn't mentioned their proposed gathering before. What was going on here?

Stephan's name came out of a crowd, called in lilting feminine tones. He shrugged, flashed Spring another of his charming smiles, and raced off with a ''Later.''

''Guess I should go, too,'' Kevin said, gazing reluctantly after his buddy.

''Don't let us keep you,'' Chad said.

''I'll be fine, Kevin,'' Spring said. She loosened her arm from his hold. ''Thanks for being my bookend.''

''Okay. See ya on Monday, Chad. Spring, how 'bout taking in a movie one night this week?''

''Um…maybe,'' she called after him.

They moved forward, sometimes dodging other

skaters by a hair, until they'd caught up with Honor and her friend half a block away.

Leilani introduced her brothers, one older and one younger. Somewhere, they'd picked up another girl they knew. The five teens began a tag game, swirling in and out until Chad growled at them to slow down before they knocked someone over.

"We promise to watch out," Honor responded as she sped out from under reaching fingers. Her infectious giggle floated over her shoulder. "I love my new wheels, Chad."

Spring smiled and glanced at Chad. The youngster was having a great time. A hobby to build on, that's for sure.

But *she* was gaining a blister.

"I've had about all the wheels I want for now. Can we sit a moment? I definitely have a learning curve here."

They found a grassy rise near the street. Spring gratefully sank down, her feet feeling like lead anchors. She pulled off her skates, rested back on her hands and wiggled her toes. Chad dug into his backpack and pulled out their shoes before unlacing his.

"When did the Peebles call with their invitation?" she asked slowly.

"Talked to Walter from the office on Friday," he replied. "It came up in passing. Just forgot to mention it, I guess." He handed her sneakers over. "Sorry."

Spring took her sneakers, but she was in no hurry

to put them on. She lay them in the grass beside her. "Did he really include me in the asking?"

"Yes, certainly. Here—I'll carry these." He took her skates and shoved them into the backpack, arranging them to fit with his. "Don't you want to go?"

"Well, sure, I guess. But it seems...I don't know—we appear too much like we're family lately. I thought you wanted to avoid that. Doesn't it seem a little odd to people? To be carting your housekeeper around with you everywhere?"

Setting the backpack aside, Chad pulled his knees up, wrapping his arms around his legs, and watched the parade of people strolling, running, or skating past them. He seemed thoughtful.

"It's a...an unusual situation, Spring, I'll grant you that. And you know very well you're not just a housekeeper. You and Honor Suzanne became friends before I got home. As a team, remember? I'm the tagalong, it seems. At church. Outings."

Was that a plaintive note she heard in his voice?

Spring cleared her throat. "You and Honor seemed to get along just fine without me the day you went to Bear Mountain."

"Yeah. Sure." He nodded. "But Honor feels more comfortable with you around."

"She'll outgrow that, given a little more time." She laid her hand on his arm, wanting to give him assurance. "You're doing great at spending more time with her. It will all smooth out."

Chad moved slightly, just enough to shake off her touch. He paused, a fleeting look of regret hovering in his eyes. Then he busied himself by buckling the straps on the backpack. Finally, he looked at her.

"How about you, Spring? Are you getting tired of being tied down? Do you want to move on?"

The breath went out of her. Why would he ask that?

"Not yet. I—I quite like having the best of two worlds. I'm not in any rush, really."

His mouth seemed to relax. "Okay. Put your shoes on and let's go."

Chapter Twelve

The evening with the Peebles was pleasant, relaxed, and full of teasing camaraderie. Chad found it amazing how well Spring fit into the family dynamics. Perhaps he shouldn't have been—she'd been proving her worth in a number of places.

And then the next few days flew past, as Spring worked to complete the wedding finery and he immersed himself in work. Spring and Honor were gone for Autumn's wedding before he had time to catch his breath.

They were gone for six days. Chad dropped back into his old habits. He indulged in a long lunch with Jonathan Feathers, then stayed late at the office, eating take-out that night. He used Saturday for catch-up, then attended a party that totally bored him.

He left the party early, wondering just why he'd consented to go. Once, he'd found the hostess the epitome of excitement and sophistication. No longer. And he found the party too noisy. He felt jaded.

Yet when he did return to his apartment, it seemed too quiet. He let out a long breath. He wasn't sure what he wanted anymore. What made him happy. He still loved his work, was content in his career. But ever since he got back from Europe—disregarding the changes in his home—his life just seemed out of balance.

Since he got back from Europe? No…it had begun before that. When his father died? Or even earlier?

He gave it up, watched the news and went to bed.

Man, was the apartment ever silent.

On Tuesday afternoon when Honor and Spring were due home, he made a point of leaving the office an hour early. No one would want to cook after a long day, he decided; he made reservations for an early dinner at one of his favorite restaurants.

He heard Honor's chatter the moment he opened the apartment door, and grinned. It had to be part of the teenage code, he thought, to have a phone glued to the ear. From her nonstop, colorful descriptions of the Truman Library and shopping on Kansas City's Country Club Plaza, he guessed she was busy filling Leilani's ears.

Spring's large shoulder bag, in which she'd taken the wedding clothes, lay where it had been dropped at the edge of the foyer. He picked it up and carried it to her bedroom door.

She lay on her bed staring at the ceiling, her hands stretched out to her sides. Her shapely calves, encased in skin-toned panty hose, dangled over the edge. The light knit dress she wore stopped at her knees. Inches beneath her feet, one shoe lay tumbled on the floor.

She didn't look up. Or acknowledge his presence.

"Want this in the closet?"

"Yes, please."

He hung it, then glanced around the room that used to be his study. It had definitely taken on feminine frills, he saw. A patterned turquoise bedspread now covered the bed, and extra pillows added; he recalled the plain navy one he'd placed there for the first housekeeper. Several pictures took pride of place on the low dresser. Her sewing machine took up the far corner, neatly contained now. She'd made the room her own. It even had her fragrance.

He turned back to gaze at Spring. She hadn't moved. She had dark half-moons under her eyes, evidence of little sleep. Her lovely mouth drooped. Had she been crying?

He'd never seen her cry. In fact, she was usually irrepressibly cheerful.

"Are you okay?"

"Sure, I'm fine." She sat up. "Only tired."

Her tentative smile looked a little tremulous. She was more than a little tired, he mused. A little down, too?

That would be natural, he supposed. He remembered his mom saying once that even happy events sometimes brought on a letdown.

He'd always heard twins were especially close, as well. And he knew Spring talked almost daily with her sister. Now that Autumn was married, that probably would change. Was Spring feeling left out? Sorry she'd come back to New York?

"Thanks," she added, and stood, seeming to shake off her mood.

Or hiding it. He wondered if he should press the issue. Would she even tell him?

"About dinner—" she began.

"Never mind. I thought we'd go out." He shoved his hands in his pockets. "Unless you'd rather stay in?"

"Oh, no..." She brushed her hair back, her hand delicate, her nails sporting a light pink polish. "I'll just change, if you don't mind."

Chad nodded, and started out of her room.

From her bedroom, they heard Honor say, "I'll get my film into an overnight developer and hopefully have 'em with me tomorrow. You'll never believe how much Spring and Autumn are alike. And Spring looked totally awesome in her maid of honor dress."

Chad stopped in the doorway and turned. If they went out, Honor would badger Spring into stopping at the overnight photo shop and whatever else entered her head.

"On the other hand, I'd just as soon stay in myself," he said. "What do you say to Chinese?"

"Sounds just right," she answered. Her gaze flashed grateful thanks, and this time her smile reflected her usual good spirits.

Satisfied with his intuitive guess, he went to greet his sister.

Ten minutes later, he punched the button on his answering machine for messages as he searched his desk for the menu from their favorite Chinese restaurant.

"Chad, I'm so-o-o disappointed you left early on Saturday night," Melissa cooed back at him. "The party was just getting started. Some of us went on to that new place with the comedy improvisations. Chad, darling, I've missed you all spring. Am I to be deprived of your company for the summer, too? Give me a call, will you?"

The machine clicked off. He let it go; he didn't think he'd be seeing Melissa again.

"Any specific requests?" he called, reading the menu as he turned.

Spring stood in the doorway, her gaze speculative. Had she heard that message? Why should it bother him if she had? Melissa had left messages before. Besides, there was no reason to keep his dating life a secret. He was a single, eligible bachelor.

But for some totally ridiculous reason that eluded him, he felt he wanted to offer an explanation.

"Melissa has a business connection with our

firm," he said with a shrug. "She likes to ask me out to enhance her social calendar."

"Mmm..." came the nondescript response from Spring. "Cashew chicken?"

Then it dawned on him; he hadn't had a real social life since he'd returned from Europe. But he now had a home life. In fact, his whole existence revolved around his work and these two young women who shared his apartment.

For Spring, settling back into her New York routine felt comfortable enough. Though she was thrilled to see her sister so deliriously happy, and enjoyed her contact with friends from home, she realized her home was no longer in Kansas City.

She accompanied Honor to ballet class the next day, picked up Chad's cleaning and shopped for dinner.

She also pulled out her list of designers she'd come to New York to gain an interview with. She went down her list once more. She underlined the top three, nationally known names she'd give anything to work for and study under. And then she sighed. It was time to make the rounds again, but she didn't feel as hopeful as she once had, given the lack of response she'd gotten so far.

If she didn't find a place with one she liked by September, perhaps she'd move to Paris. She had enough money from her inheritance to last a couple of years there, if she stretched it.

Chad came home on time for dinner the rest of the week. He usually buried himself in work after dinner, but on Thursday night he joined her and Honor in a board game. Honor chatted about what she needed for camp the next week. They were to leave first thing on Monday morning.

"I don't have a flashlight," she muttered. "And my sleeping bag got left in Virginia."

"Don't worry about it," Chad said. "Give me a list, and I'll get everything you need tomorrow during lunch."

"You won't know exactly what I want," she complained. "You'll get it all wrong—or something completely dorky."

"Then I promise you the three of us will do the shopping together on Saturday," he insisted. But he let Spring see his amusement, winking to include her. "Just don't go bouncing off the walls before Monday, okay?"

"Okay. Can Leilani come for an overnight this weekend?"

"What? She's not going to camp with you?"

"Well, yeah. What's your point?"

"Aargh," he teased with a dramatic hand against his head. "I'm drowning in teen clumping."

"'Clumping!' Well, next week you won't have any teens around at all. I won't be here."

True, Spring thought, flashing a glance toward Chad. They'd be alone in the apartment. His gaze skittered away, and he changed the subject.

On Friday, rain came in, hard and drenching. The TV weatherman promised it would last the weekend. Honor groaned. "Oh, please, please, let the weather be good for camp," she wailed.

Looking for something to occupy Honor until Monday, Spring visited the video store on Saturday morning. She rented two old costume movies, and checked out history and costume books from the library on the same time period. At the second-hand clothing store, she found a long feather and two long skirts, one a blue satin and the other a printed cotton.

Leilani came for a sleep-over, and the girls dressed up and paraded about the apartment while Spring roasted a chicken. She served it early, with baked potatoes and whole baked onions, a basket of fruit and hunks of French bread. Beside each paper plate, she placed a single small sharp knife.

"This is the best I can do at imitating an average table of that time," she said.

They laughed their way through dinner, with Chad pretending courtly behavior. When they settled down to watch the movies, Chad read them a quick survey of seventeenth- and eighteenth-century French history.

"Later, we can get into both the American and then the French Revolution," he said, gaining enthusiasm for the task. "Those were wildly changing times. And we can visit more than West Point to get a sense of how our country developed. A weekend jaunt can take us to quite a few significant spots."

Spring glanced at him, her clear eyes seeming to ask when that would be, and perhaps even asking if those jaunts would include her. It struck him that he wanted them to, intended the outing for all of them. But would that be wise?

He let the book drop to his lap, muttering, "Hit the play button." He definitely needed a distraction from his troubling thoughts.

They were about to leave church the next morning when Dana caught Spring on the front steps. "Spring?"

She turned, Chad and Honor pausing to wait for her a few feet away. "Hi, Dana. Good service this morning. I loved the special music."

"Yes, that's a lovely group." Dana glanced at Chad and Honor, then said, "Hey, I've run into a glitch for camp next week. We've had a couple of emergencies, and we're in desperate need of a couple more counselors for this week. Can you go? Most parents or anyone qualified have to work."

"But Dana, I'm not qualified. I, um…do work. You know my situation."

Chad stepped up. "What's the problem?"

"Dana needs another counselor for this week's camp."

"Chad, I realize you pay Spring a salary to maintain your household, but it really would help me out if you'd let her go. Actually, we're in desperate need of three counselors. You can't imagine all the problems that have come up this week, I—'' she pulled in a great breath, shifting a stack of magazines and boxes she carried ''—rather, Josh Nolan and I have racked our brains and gone over church lists to fill in these last-minute gaps, but we've come up with no one who can fill them. Except Spring.''

''Yes, but Dana, I'm not…well, I've learned to love the Bible teachings and I believe them wholly, but I'm not an experienced Bible authority or anything like that,'' Spring protested. ''Besides, I've been a part of the church such a short time. Someone might object.''

''Uh-huh, I realize that. But no one could object to your serving in the kitchen. Then you could relieve Jessica Tailor to teach one of the Bible sessions. And we need you to bunk in with one cabin, too.''

''Well, I'd be willing, I guess…'' Spring turned to look at Chad.

Chad didn't even hesitate. ''Sure. Go along, Spring. You work hard enough to earn your salary, regardless.''

''Oh, Chad, you're a lifesaver,'' Dana gushed. ''God bless you! Now, if only I could replace my boys' swimming instructor, I'd be convinced God's glitches were only His sense of humor all along.''

''Dana, Chad can swim really well,'' Honor began, her face full of enthusiasm.

''No, you don't, Honor Suzanne,'' Chad instantly responded. ''Don't go there.''

"But you do, Chad, don't deny it." Honor turned to Dana. "Honest, Dana, he won races and stuff when he was in high school—"

"Honor," Chad protested. "I'm not a teacher."

"—and college," Honor continued in spite of his protest. "Dad had his ribbons. He showed them to Mom and me many times. He was so proud of Chad."

Their father had talked of him to Sandra? Had shown his few ribbons to her and Honor?

"Is there any way possible you could come and serve our camp for the week?" Dana's gaze was full of hope and pleading. "It pays nothing in money, I'm afraid, but reams and reams in satisfaction and spiritual growth, and often lasting friendships."

Actually, he had vacation time coming. He hadn't used all of his allotted time for several years running.

"Only one week, Chad," Honor begged. "The Pocono Mountains are really pretty, everyone says."

"Well, I've never taught anyone to swim before, and I haven't visited the gym in months, now, as it happens."

He glanced meaningfully at the members of his household. Honor simply shrugged. Spring folded her lips, but her eyes sparkled with merriment.

He glared. They weren't helping him a whit. So his excuse sounded a little too lame—was that any way to help a family member out?

"But you could teach it if you had to, Chad." His

sister was on a roll. "And you passed lifesaving in school, didn't you? Where's the problem?"

"The problem, Honor Suzanne, is that I'm not teacher material. It wouldn't be fair to force all those kids to suffer with my impatience. I'd expect too much from them."

"God be praised, that's just the kind of counselor we need, Chad," Dana said.

Beside her, Honor pressed her hands together in a plea. Spring's mouth quivered. Her chin lowered and she flashed him one glance upward through her lashes.

She was *laughing!*

He let her feel the full force of his glare.

"As you must know," Dana explained, "we have kids from all backgrounds going, most of whom need a firm hand. There're only six boys to a cabin. You'd be responsible at night to only those..."

Only six?

"...most of the time."

What was this "most of the time"?

"There's a permanent staff who take care of the grounds and buy supplies, but we have to furnish all the other personnel. Another church group will be there the same time as we are, and they'll be responsible for giving us a couple of adults, too. But we're by far the largest church going. We'll have to cut our list of kids if we don't have the full complement of adults."

"Couldn't I just work in the kitchen like Spring?"

he asked, caving in. Honor squealed, while Spring's mouth curved into a full grin. "And be with the kids only at night?"

"And teach swimming?" Dana pushed.

He let out an exasperated sigh. "All right. But I'll need some help."

"I'll see what I can do." Dana raced away.

"Let's go find brunch," Honor said. "I'm starved."

"Wait just a minute, young lady. You got us into this. Now we have to scramble to find what Spring and I will need for this, uh, camp."

"Oh, yeah," Honor said, all too innocent. "Well, um, I'm sure Dana or Josh can help us out. They said—"

"Honor Suzanne, you sneaky little mouse! You knew Dana was going to ask me to help out with camp before she asked, didn't you?" Spring said.

"Not before this morning, I promise you," Honor said with a chuckle. "But I did think it might work out."

"My sister, the traitor!" Chad spoke through gritted teeth. He reached for her with outstretched hands and stiffly curled fingers, as if pretending he'd strangle her.

Honor giggled and dashed away down the street.

"And I have years of this to look forward to?" He rolled his eyes as they strolled to follow, then grinned at Spring. "What have I gotten myself into?"

Chapter Thirteen

Chad spent about forty minutes on the phone. His longest call was to Anne. She could handle the rearrangement of most of his working schedule, and take care of a couple of minor matters on her own. He'd have to postpone a meeting with Jonathan, but would make that call himself, he told her.

"Oh, Chad, before you go, what do you want to do about that Association dinner? Accept or bow out?"

He leaned back in his chair and thought a moment. He should accept. The evening, though mostly social, still held a lot of business prestige. Melissa and her crowd would be there. It might be prudent for him to take a date.

From Spring's bedroom where a major search and weed-out packing operation was going on, came a sudden burst of giggles. A second later, he watched

Spring stroll through the living room on her way to the kitchen, her laughter trailing behind.

She looked trim and attractive in the pink suit she'd worn to church. Her hair swung free as she turned slightly to answer one of Honor's questions. It brushed her shoulders softly.

All at once, he recalled how soft her hair had felt against his hands the night he'd kissed her. How it had felt against his lips. How it smelled—like her name. Like spring blossoms.

"Chad, are you there?"

"Uh, yeah, sure, Anne." He cleared his throat. "I was just thinking about that dinner. Yes, make reservations for two in my name, please..."

His gaze dropped to Spring's bare feet: pretty feet, with a lovely arch.

Blinking, he jerked his head around to stare at the wall behind his desk. Having two young women in his home was entirely too distracting at times. Especially when one wasn't his sister.

But he couldn't take Spring to that dinner. She was in his employ. How would that look? He could imagine the gossip such an event would cause around the office water-cooler, and there had been enough of that already after their afternoon of skating. Kevin had slyly hinted he wanted to date Spring, but he hesitated to create difficulties for Chad.

Chad had barely prevented himself from snarling when he replied that Spring was free to date whomever she wanted. Why didn't Kevin call her? he suggested.

He didn't think Spring had heard from him, but he wasn't about to ask her.

He pursed his mouth. Talking business law wasn't Spring's world. She'd be bored if he took her to that dinner. Anne would know how to mix and mingle with the corporate crowd. Talk their lingo.

Anne was closer to his own age.

He took the plunge and played on Anne's ambition to move up in the firm. "And if you don't mind, make plans to be my dinner partner, will you? I don't think there will be other members of our firm available to go. It's time you stepped up your efforts for the firm if you hope to make associate next year."

"You mean it?" came the enthusiastic response. "Yes, of course, I'll attend with you. I'm happy to help represent the firm. Thanks for the opportunity, Chad."

That settled, he called Jonathan Feathers at his home in Connecticut.

"Sure, take the week off, Chad," Jonathan answered when he explained the situation. "Now that I'm back in the saddle for the summer, I expect we can field anything that comes up from your desk. Anne's on top of things, isn't she?"

"Yes, she certainly is." Chad knew Jonathan had a fondness for Anne, and now praised her work.

"And how're things working out at home?" Jonathan enquired. "You're going to chaperone your young sister at camp, you say?"

"That's the general idea, I guess. But I got roped into this thing to teach swimming and to monitor one of the boys' cabins at night."

Jonathan laughed. "Good. Good. Won't hurt you a bit. Test your mettle in new ways. Biggest challenge of long-term corporations is to find new perspectives on life. Keeps your mind sharp, so to speak."

"Yes, sir."

"That's why I love theater. My wife and I support our local amateur theater groups, you know. Completely different from the law. Doesn't go stale that way."

"Yeah, I know. Are you still invested in the city?" For some years, Jonathan Feathers, who was known to have deep pockets, had been a soft touch for a new production. He often sponsored young artists, as well.

"No. No, but I keep my contacts, just in case something should come up that I like. Say, Chad, about our London connection..."

They eventually closed their conversation with an agreement to have dinner together one day soon after Chad's return from camp.

"Meant to see more of you after your jaunt in Europe, but it seems too many irons in the fire means it takes time to keep 'em hot."

"Yes, that it does, sir."

Chad leaned back in his chair as he mulled over his client list. Nothing else needed his immediate attention, he was pleased to note. He'd delegated what he could to Anne. Jonathan would field some of his cases this week. The two Sanders brothers handled a different line in the firm, so he seldom interchanged work with them. Anything else he had could go on hold.

The firm was changing, he mused. The Sanders, Ken and Lawrence, were both of retirement age; Jonathan had called a board meeting for September, and he'd hinted that perhaps Ken, the elder of the brothers, would announce his retirement by year's end.

If the firm was to expand any further, they'd need to bring even more attorneys on board. Perhaps Anne Martin wouldn't be the only new associate; Kevin Jensen was ready.

"Chad, we've found an old sleeping bag in the back of your storage closet," Honor called, bringing his attention back to matters at hand.

"What are you doing digging around in my closet?" The bag was one he'd used in college. He'd forgotten it was there.

He rose and went to stand in his bedroom door. Honor was half hidden inside a huge box.

"Helping you pack" came Honor's reply. She pushed the box back into the closet, then picked up a stack of T-shirts she'd pulled out of a chest. "These will do, I suppose."

"You don't think I can take care of that?"

"It's been a long time since you had to live around a bunch of kids, Chad. I want to make sure you're prepared."

"Are you implying I've forgotten what it is to be a teen?"

"Well, no offence, Chad. But you're *thirty-four*..."

"Brat! You think thirty-four is *old?*" His first instinct was to tickle her, as he'd done when she was little on those rare occasions that he'd visited their Virginia home. But she wasn't a small child anymore.

He swung around to face Spring, loitering in her own doorway. He tipped his head as though asking what she had to say to that. "Can you believe this brash child? She has the nerve to call me *old.*"

"Um...not me," Spring said with a teasing grin and a shrug.

"And I don't want you to embarrass me with the wrong clothes," Honor added.

"Watch it. Now you're stomping on my ego. This old man may just have to dunk you when we find the camp pool!"

"Providing you can catch me," she said, making a superior face, then following up with a giggle.

"I can see we're in for quite a week," Chad said on a groan. "Days of this ahead, swamped in teenage mentality. What brainpower! Is there no hope? Can't you get me out of this?"

"Don't look at me," Spring said again. "You're on your own."

"Oh, you won't help me out?" He gave her a half-grin, noticing for the thousandth time how delightfully her mouth curved when she smiled.

"I have my own packing to do," she returned smartly, and disappeared into her room.

They left at dawn the next day from the church parking lot.

For Spring, the next week was a revelation. She and Autumn had never been to camp. Her sister's disabling fear of crowds was the main reason, she supposed, and then Uncle William had kept them close to home, in any case.

The long ride south to Pennsylvania on the church bus was an adventure in itself. Chad followed in his car, but Spring felt honor-bound to travel with the kids and Dana. Josh Nolan and a couple of other adults were in a second bus. Four other adults, Dana told her, including her husband, Claude, the church's associate pastor, were traveling down later that day for two days. But Claude had duties at the church and couldn't stay any longer.

Spring laughed and talked with the teens around her, listened to their jokes and teasing, and stumbled off the vehicle gratefully after the bus pulled up hours later to a lodge in a wooded clearing.

Almost immediately, Honor disappeared with Leilani and a handful of others, to go exploring. Dana ordered them to return in five minutes; they had to be responsible for their own things, she insisted. They also had to get their cabin assignments.

"Some of these kids are still learning that we don't provide servants here at camp," she grumped. "Won't they be surprised to find they have to make their own beds!" Then she smiled. "And some of them will learn what it is to *be* a servant while they're here. Camp gives most kids a new look at serving God, and us grown-ups a chance to experience it."

Serving God...

Spring had never equated that term with herself before. If she'd had any thoughts about the matter, she supposed, she'd thought it meant sequestering oneself away from society for prayer and contemplation for the rest of one's life. But Dana and Claude Bates served the church with all their energy, visions and faith. She knew for a fact that Dana was involved with both the soup kitchen and building the youth ministry. She kept regular counseling hours, too, putting her degree to work. If a kid or a family needed her, she was there in a flash. Josh Nolan and others of the church staff did likewise. But was that what the term meant?

Dana had often spoken of her love for God, for Jesus, and talked of the Holy Spirit as if intimately acquainted with Him. So had Josh.

And young Honor never ended her day without a prayer. Spring had felt like an intruder when she'd first overheard her young friend. Then Honor had invited her to share in the prayers, and, slowly, she'd come to feel included in them. But was that enough to serve God?

Jenny Bloom and Tina Higgins, the other two female volunteers, came back from talking with the camp director. "We have only an hour to settle in," Jenny said. Thin and constantly on the go, she added, "I was hoping for a nap."

"No such luck, ladies," Josh said, coming up to them. "After lunch in that screened building just there—" he pointed to the nearby structure "—we have our opening assembly in the stadium over that hill. Now let's get this check-in done."

The camp was divided into three sections; the boys were lodged in the blue zone, while the girls were lodged in the red zone. Small cabins could be spotted left and right through the woods. Blue, red and yellow signs posted the territories.

"Who lives in the yellow zone?" Chad said just above her ear as they stood in line to get their assignments. "The cowards?"

"Possibly," Dana answered, overhearing. "The permanent staff have those cabins."

"Figures." Chad nodded sagely. The line moved up a pace. They moved with it.

"Well, if I'm to help in the kitchen..." Spring began, raising a brow and moving forward. The yellow zone cabins, immediately behind the check-in building, looked to be much larger than the ones housing the students. The swimming pool hugged close behind, too.

"No, you don't get off that easy, pal." Dana was good-natured but firm. "I need you close to me."

Spring laughed. The line moved up again. "All right. I don't really want to be in with strangers, anyway."

"Me, either," Chad muttered. "But shouldn't I be housed closer to the pool, Miss Dana?"

"Uh-uh. Play fair. You promised to help Josh out with the guys."

"So I did," he said. They'd reached the head of the line. "Okay, Josh. Which cabin?"

The next five days fell into place, with morning activities, afternoon swims, crafts, music and drama and Bible study. They hiked, wrote their own plays based on Bible issues, and listened each evening as Josh gave an illustration of a different parable.

Chad felt as though he'd stepped back in time. He recalled several summers filled with church camp, Boy Scout camp, and a few years of family camping. Wonderful memories, he thought.

This time was different. As one of the adults in charge of keeping a strict eye on a string of teenage boys with jumping hormones, he needed to be alert at all times. Especially when they interacted with the girls. *All* the girls.

And the girls were little better. He thought his eyes might spring a muscle trying to observe his sister, too. She seemed taken with a tall boy whom he'd never met, and she and Leilani made it a point to sit near him each chance they got.

Yet he found himself looking for Spring more than anyone else throughout the day. At mealtime, she'd come around with platters of food, her hair in a high ponytail. Some of the older boys tried flirting with her. She kidded them back, keeping it above questionable expressions or double meanings. Chad thought her quite skillful.

He found himself hanging around to talk to her after his swim sessions were over and his class had gone on to another activity. Late afternoons were when some of the office and other off-duty staff members came for a dip in the pool. Spring wore a modest blue swimsuit, and swam a few laps before getting out, her hair sleek against her head. She hurried to dry off and run back to her cabin to change.

He teased her sometimes. Worked at making her laugh. He couldn't help himself. In the evenings, he gravitated to her side like a bird to trees. He watched for her to finish her chores and leave the dining room. When she hurried to find a place in the giant semicircle just as Josh began to speak at the rustic outdoor stadium, he scooted aside to make a place for her. And beckoned her to sit beside him.

Honor naturally hung with her friends. He always knew where she was in the bleachers, even among the nearly two hundred kids present. But he also noted that Spring always paused to spot his sister among the crowd before climbing to where he sat toward the top.

The first evening Spring took her seat with a quick, glowing smile. She'd forgotten her Bible, and had no time to get it. Chad opened his, and they read the passages together.

Josh read and explained the events surrounding how Jesus gave the "Parable of the Sower."

"Guys and girls, I tell you that Jesus says you're here to listen." Josh held his open Bible high. He walked back and forth, his earnestness to make his point giving his rugged face an authority Chad hadn't noticed before. "Open your ears to hear.

"You can decide right this moment what kind of soil you will be. Hard? Rocky? Choked with weeds? Or are you good black-growing dirt? Ready to produce a crop. A healthy crop blossoming and growing, heavy with fruit. See, kids, Jesus tells us that we, all of mankind, reflect those kinds of human conditions. He gives us the Word. The good news. Love our God with all our being. Love our neighbors as ourselves.

"But he gives us the freedom to choose. Are we going to give up our Christian walk when we run into a rocky place? When we become angry or disillusioned? When the world gets tough on us? Do we whine and say that we're not treated fair? Quit talking with God? Drop out of church? Or do we shore up the soil and care for our souls with God's Word?"

Chad felt struck with an arrow of truth. He'd dropped out of church after leaving home. Oh, not right away. His emotional departure had begun slowly, after his mom died. He'd developed spiritual erosion without knowing just when it happened.

When had he left God behind?

Ah, Father, forgive me. I didn't intend to ignore You. But I let my relationship with You slip. Help me to regain my heart for You... Help me to be the kind of brother to Honor Suzanne that she needs. And to come to terms with the feelings I'm starting to have for Spring...

Beside him, Chad felt her move. Her arm brushed his, her skin warm and vibrant. He watched her profile as she listened intently to Josh's every word.

She straightened, stretching to sit taller as if her back felt tired. As Cook's assistant, he knew she was up at five o'clock each morning. She put in long days here. Dare he put an arm around her? Couldn't he merely place his arm just behind her to give her a little support without it appearing too intimate?

Guide me, Lord. Guide me....

Chapter Fourteen

Chad's duties as a swimming instructor were cut short on Friday afternoon. The kids were out on a final hike, but were expected back to camp headquarters just before suppertime. Afterward, they'd have their last campfire talk. They'd leave for home about mid-afternoon tomorrow.

The late afternoon buzzed with inertia. Spring didn't show up for her usual swim, and neither did any of the staff. Chad went to find her.

He opened the dining room screened door and let it slap closed behind him. Overhead, the fans whirred in the afternoon heat. Air-conditioning was not an accommodation the camp provided, even in the kitchen and dining room.

He strolled toward the kitchen area, semi-closed off from the dining hall by a wall and buffet counter.

Only Spring and the cook were there. She was busy dicing cooked potatoes.

"Oh, hi, Chad." She looked up. "What's going on?"

"You didn't make it over for a swim today," he remarked.

"Nope. Cook lost two helpers this morning. Dentist's visit and a car repair. So we're shorthanded in the kitchen this evening and tomorrow."

"Oh. Well, couldn't you get any other help?"

She glanced up a him. A slow smile began and spread. Above it, her eyes twinkled. "Not until now…"

"Not me."

"Why not? You have a capable pair of hands. No injuries. No sprains. Are you sure you know what you're asking for?"

"Did I offer to help?"

"Um, no, but you're here." The humor in her gaze increased. "And free for a few hours."

"I didn't say I was free, did I? I charge quite a lot for my services, I'll have you know. And what if I have something else to do?"

"You don't, do you?"

"Well, there are several things I *could* do."

"Aw, c'mon, Chad. It'll be fun." She handed him a paper towel and pointed him toward the sink to wash his hands. "Think of it as another way of serving the Lord. You'll have a chance to see how the other half lives."

"You are an odd woman to find fun in kitchen work."

"It's not that I find fun in the work itself," she said, returning her attention to the industrial-size pan of potatoes she was assembling with chopped egg, celery and pickles. "It's that I find fun in the results. Now with dress design, I have fun from the first concept to the last—making it come alive in the finished product. But working this week in camp has been a lot of fun."

"Fun..." He shook his head. "Okay. What do you want me to do?"

"Oh, Cook's in charge. His name's Ed."

The cook, a middle-aged man with grizzled looks, had been a career Navy cook. He gave Chad a hard once-over when Spring introduced them. Chad almost saluted. Instead, he tucked his T-shirt into his tan shorts and announced he was ready to work.

"Jist call me 'Cook,'" Ed said.

"Well, Spring says you need an extra pair of hands."

"Sure, mister. Chad, is it? Stack them plates, why don'tcha?" He jerked his chin toward the stainless steel counters and appliances. Two dishwashers still held the lunch dishes. Cook turned back to attend the huge grill, adjusting the knobs. "And fill the silverware buckets. Then ya can get them platters down for Little Bit, here." He jerked his chin toward Spring. "She ain't tall 'nough to reach 'em."

"Little Bit?" Chad raised a brow, not even trying to cover his teasing grin.

Spring tipped her chin up and lifted a shoulder, as though to say, *"So what if the cook wants to call me a child's name?"*

"Then git out them chicken pieces," Cook continued, giving their byplay little notice.

Chad glanced around. *Chicken pieces?*

Spring tipped her head toward the stainless steel refrigerator, and he opened the huge doors. Inside, he found industrial-size packages of pieces of chicken. Gallons of coleslaw sat in stainless steel containers there.

"Hop to, mates," Cook clipped out. "Them kids'll be in here in less'n an hour, hungrier'n a whole shipload o' sailors comin' off shore leave."

Chad jumped to follow directions. He got paper napkins from the storage supply cupboard and set up the cafeteria-style counter, while Spring mixed a vat of potato salad.

"These here dishwashers c'n be unloaded," Cook said, giving him no slack. "Don't want nothin' in the way when we get supper over."

"Gotcha," Chad answered.

Spring pulled dishes from the dishwasher racks and passed them to him over the serving counter. His hands tangled with hers as she handed over bunches of forks and spoons. He dropped a few, making a *clang* on the concrete floor.

He uttered a disgruntled noise. Spring merely

laughed, the sound pelting him softly as she came around the counter.

His irritation fled. Flashing her a grin in return, he realized for the first time that she seldom showed any real irritation. So far, he'd never seen her even terribly annoyed. What would it take to raise her ire?

He dumped the flatware he still held in the crocks used as containers, then bent to help her pick up what had fallen on the floor. Under the table, she spotted a crumpled napkin, left from lunch.

"Oh, bother. No one had time to really sweep after lunch. Put these back in the dishwasher," she said, handing him the ones she'd picked up. "I'll get a broom."

"Don't have no time for sweepin' now," Cook grumped.

"I'll just give it a lick and a promise," Spring insisted. She opened one of the long cupboards against the far wall in the rectangular dining room opposite the kitchen, to pull out a push broom.

"Lick 'n' a promise." Cook never took his gaze from the five-gallon pot he was using to flour-coat the chicken. "Ain't heard that'n in ages."

Neither had Chad. He dredged up the memory of his grandmother's firm hand during a summer visit when he was eight, telling him he had to give his face a better wash than "a lick and a promise."

Looking at Spring's well-scrubbed face, he captured her gaze with his own. He had an instant urge to give her lovely face a...promise. More than a promise.

Holding the push broom, as tall as she, Spring paused and closed the cupboard door, as though in slow motion. Her eyes darkened to a marine blue.

That sense of promise hung between them with the very air they breathed. Warm. Close. And fragrant with the smells of frying chicken and the sweet wild roses that some of the kids had placed on the oilcloth-covered picnic tables.

Cook rattled a pan.

Chad turned away and swallowed. "My grandmother used to use that expression."

"Oh, my neighbor used it all the time," Spring said brightly. Very brightly, before yanking her gaze back to the floor in front of her broom. She'd practically stumbled over it when she'd turned to find Chad looking at her. "Autumn and I used to collect as many of the old sayings as we could. They're a lot of fun and sometimes say just what a person really wants to say."

Chad noticed the rosy glow that suddenly crept up her cheeks.

Spring shoved the broom in front of her as she crossed the floor. Chad lifted a handful of chairs, letting her make a quick sweep, then found the dustpan. As they worked in unison for a full five minutes without talk, Chad couldn't help wondering how deep Spring's sweet nature went.

He dropped to his heels to offer the dustpan. She meticulously swept every last crumb into it.

His gaze traveled upward, taking in her slender form. Drifting higher, he found her gaze waiting for his. She seemed incapable of looking elsewhere. Her mouth parted.

Chad thought her lips seemed to grow more enticing and softer with each indrawn breath. He wanted to kiss her. He *really* wanted to kiss her.

If they hadn't had an audience, he would have.

The broom beneath her hand slowed.

He recalled how sweet she'd felt once before, how warm and responsive.

Could this woman possibly be as giving and as unselfish as she appeared? He sincerely doubted those traits existed strongly in anyone, any longer. If they did, there was usually an expected payback lurking around a corner.

How long could she keep it up, if she wasn't sincere? For the rest of the summer?

What did Spring really want in life? She talked of studying dress design, but so far he thought her efforts to find a job with a New York designer rather limp.

Maybe she needed a little push. Someone to believe in her talent.

He knew nothing about the field, but her clothing choices often reflected a freshness that pleased him. And his glimpse of the wedding dress she'd made for her sister had certainly been impressive.

Was she really talented?

Did it matter?

Maybe he ought to find out. He'd hate to see her languish for want of a little self-confidence.

Yet, talent wasn't enough in today's world. Success in any field demanded drive and ambition and incredible luck. Especially in New York. And sometimes—more likely than not—good contacts.

Good contacts...

A distant shout told them the hungry hordes were only yards down the trail. It was the start of the ten-minute countdown.

Chad abruptly stood as he pushed his thoughts aside in favor of the task at hand.

Spring felt as worn-out as a dishcloth by the time the three of them dragged through the lobby of their apartment building on Saturday night. Their buses had been late in arriving, and although Spring thought longingly of a ride back in the comfort of Chad's car, she felt committed to stay with the kids; Dana would need her. They were the last to leave the campground.

Chad reached the church more than an hour earlier than the buses. He hung around to bring them home.

Lester, their forty-something building super, was ambling through the building lobby when they arrived, his hips saddled low with a wide leather tool belt. He and his wife shared the basement apartment with an assortment of relatives.

"Hi, Lester," Chad said. "Aren't you off duty?"

"S'posed to be, but you know how it goes."

"Yeah, actually, I do. Wouldn't want to earn an extra twenty, would you?"

"Puttin' your car away?" Lester asked. They'd been through such an arrangement before, and Chad always gave him a great Christmas tip, as well. "Sure, I'll do it."

"Thanks, buddy." He flipped Lester his keys. His garage was only half a block away—an easy jog back.

The girls held the elevator for him.

"Uh, by the way," Lester said as he paused to hitch up his belt. "There was a guy here looking for Miss Barbour."

"Who was it?" Spring asked.

"Said he was a friend of yours from home."

Spring stepped out of the elevator. "Did he give you his name, Lester?"

"Nope. Said he'd call."

"All right. Thanks."

They rode up, no one speaking. But as soon as they got through the apartment door, Honor announced, "I'm for bed. See you two in the morning, but don't wake me until ten till..."

"Ten till?" Chad queried.

"Ten minutes till time to leave for church," she explained through a mammoth yawn. She immediately disappeared into her bedroom.

Spring smothered a responsive yawn.

"Not a chance, you scamp," Chad shot back at his sister. "Thirty minutes before, at least. And that won't account for time to shampoo your hair, so if you want to do that, it's an hour earlier."

"You're a bear, Chad. Know that? But I love you a whole bunch, anyway." Honor's voice became muffled as her door closed.

"I think I'll have something cold to drink," Spring said. She headed toward the kitchen. "Do you want anything, Chad?"

"Hmm?" He stood in the tiny hall outside the bedrooms and stared at Honor's door. "Sure. A cola, if you don't mind."

He followed Spring into the kitchen, reaching for snack crackers. "Do you know, I think that's the first time Honor ever said…"

"Said what?" She glanced at him as she filled two glasses with ice.

"That she loves me."

"Didn't you know that? She does, you know. More than anyone else on this earth."

"I guess…I suppose I haven't thought much about it. My family…we loved each other, and Mom always showed it, would often say the words—but my dad never did." He shook his head. "Guess he must've been more demonstrative with Honor."

Spring handed him his glass of cola, then leaned back against the kitchen counter.

"I always heard that fathers are a little softer with their daughters than with their sons. Giving more affection. I wouldn't know. My father left us before Autumn and I had a chance to know him. But when my mom died, we had Uncle William.''

"He's the man who raised you?" Chad wanted to keep her talking. He liked it when her voice grew soft and confiding, he realized.

He should let her go on to bed. They were both tired.

He didn't move.

"Uncle William was old-fashioned and strict, but he took great care of us. We felt loved. But…'' She frowned, staring down at her bare feet. Her shoes had been left in the front hall.

She continued. "I suppose what a child learns early in life stays with them. Honor and I share that feeling of…not abandonment, really, because neither of us has truly been abandoned. Not when Autumn and I had Uncle William. And Honor now has you.''

She glanced up at him through her lashes, a shyness showing for the first time. Chad realized her halting admission of deep emotion was a struggle.

He wanted to say something to ease her embarrassment. He wished, somehow, to erase the tag ends of old sorrow that he saw in her eyes; it caused her too much pain. He should say something.

But nothing came to mind, and his desire to know what she really felt overrode his better judgment. He leaned against the table and let her continue.

"But still—'' she spoke slowly, as though drawing the words from a deep well ''—there is a—like a leftover emotion....''

He suddenly recognized the feeling. He'd never put a label on it before. Never admitted he'd felt it. He'd thought a man simply accepted what the world dealt him, without whining. But her words uncovered his own forgotten teenage pain at losing his own mother too soon.

''Yeah... Like an unfinished piece of you. Lost.''

''Yes. That says it pretty well, I guess.'' A tentative smile flashing across her lips stole into his heart. Her eyes carried a sheen. ''And when that happens at a young age, as it did...''

Again, Spring searched for words. She'd always known her sister's childhood trauma, when Autumn had become lost in a mob of people for hours and hours before she and Mom found her again, had affected them both. How could it not? But now, for the first time, she thought perhaps she'd suffered almost as much as Autumn had.

That devastating event, followed soon after by their mother's leaving them behind, had given her more of a hole in her middle than she'd faced before. Granted, she'd hidden it better than Autumn. She'd been the take-charge sister. But she'd neglected her own needs until a few months ago, when she and Autumn had taken a healthy step toward becoming individuals.

She raised her gaze once more. She didn't know

why, but she felt it important that Chad understand what the years ahead might mean for his sister.

She stumbled to complete her thought. "When a family, for whatever reason…has a parting…for the child left behind, something inside remains…incomplete. I think one always is looking to find those missing pieces so that part of you doesn't remain lost forever. That's what Honor is looking for in staying here with you. The love factor, the nurturing. That's what she needs from you."

The love factor… Didn't everyone need love? Yet there were many kinds of love, many degrees. Of love, of desire…

Chad set his glass down. Then he took Spring's glass from her hand and put it on the counter. He cupped her chin, spreading his fingers against her soft skin, and lay his mouth against hers as he'd been waiting to do since yesterday.

He kept the kiss gentle in spite of the hot desire that quickly rose. His whole body shook with it. It flooded his mind. It would be so easy to get swept away.

A soft sound came from Spring's throat. A protest? Her own desire?

A clear, sharp thought penetrated his fogged brain. *Let her go… Desire isn't always love, and Spring deserves real love. The love of a husband.*

He pulled away and simply looked at her for a moment. She sucked in a long breath, her eyes almost clouded with answering passion.

"Good night, Spring. Thank you. Thank you for understanding Honor so well. She—we'll both gain by your wisdom."

With each step, he reminded himself how young Spring was. Too young for him to take advantage. Even so, it still took more self-control than he'd ever experienced before to walk away.

Chapter Fifteen

Chad didn't even bother to listen to the answering machine messages until the next morning. He'd been too disturbed after the encounter with Spring to do anything but go to bed. But he didn't sleep well. He'd tossed and turned, calling up now familiar arguments for remaining aloof from Spring. She was much younger than him. She hadn't had a lot of experience with men. He had no business taking advantage of her.

He had no business pursuing her when she was in his home as an employee! Such a situation would make him furious if it happened elsewhere, if Honor found herself pushed in such a way. In fact, if another man made the kind of advances he'd made toward Spring…

What should he do?

He wished he knew. He *did* find her attractive.

More than merely attractive. He had a hard time keeping his hands to himself when she was around.

Punching his pillow, he flopped over to his stomach. He'd go back and kiss her again in the next breath if...

Lord, when it comes to Spring, I don't seem to have any common sense at all...I'm completely weak. Please give me the strength I need to step away and do no harm.

The smart thing to do was ask her to leave. Yet he couldn't do that when Honor seemed to need Spring so much. Besides, Honor would question any such action, and he didn't think he was prepared to explain.

Oh, Lord, I am surely in need of you now...

When Chad did punch the answering machine the next morning, one of the messages was for Spring— a deep, eager young voice, asking her to call him. It must be her friend from Kansas City, Chad guessed. He was in town and wanted to see her. He told her the hotel at which he was staying and the number.

"Oh, Tyler!" Spring exclaimed when she heard it. Dressed in her summer robe, she'd just come from a shower, Chad noticed. Not a single blemish marred her smooth skin, not a single brush of makeup. It wasn't that he thought her the most beautiful woman he'd ever met; he merely thought her the loveliest.

From the corner of his eye, he watched her punch in the number given. Chad told himself he shouldn't listen. This was a private conversation between Spring and her friend.

Yet he hovered, taking a stack of work he'd left on his desk last week, sitting in the leather chair, shuffling though it while she talked. His mind didn't register much beyond the tabs.

"Tyler? What are you doing in New York?" She paused, looked at the desk clock. "It's eight already, and you said to call." She chuckled, listened, then chuckled again.

"I'm good. Uh-huh. Well, I suppose I could..." She turned to meet Chad's gaze. "Only the weekend? You should've let me know you were coming. I was out of town until last night."

Another pause. "Yes, that would be fun. Okay. I'll meet you in your hotel lobby at eleven."

Spring hung up. "Is it all right with you if I'm out this afternoon?"

"Sure. Of course. Why wouldn't it be?"

"I, um, just wondered if you might need me for anything."

Chad cleared his throat. "No, not at all. You run along and visit with your friend. Honor and I can find enough to fill our afternoon."

"Well, I'm not meeting him until after the service." She glanced at the clock again. "I'd better wake Honor."

They arrived for the early church service on time, though Honor grouched that she hadn't had enough time to dry her hair properly. The service was full of humor, as they shared what the week at camp had meant to the youth of their church. Clearly, many felt high with blessings.

After the laughter had died down, Spring thought how much the experience had meant to her, how much she'd learned with the nightly Bible studies. Josh had brought the parables so alive for her that she'd come away with new understanding of the Scriptures, and a deeper faith. She felt a greater inner connection to herself, to her Lord.

She'd needed all of it last night. She'd gone to bed only to wrestle with total confusion and unrequited emotions.

She'd wanted those over-the-moon kisses to go on and on…. Yet Chad had walked away, leaving her nearly in tears.

This morning, she was very glad he had. Her resistance to him had been nonexistent.

She pulled in a deep breath. There was no way she'd ever put aside what had happened between her and Chad last night. She simply didn't know what would come of it yet.

Would Chad ignore that…that *something* that pulled them together as he had the last time they'd kissed? Or would he acknowledge what they'd shared? What had he been thinking this morning? He'd barely looked at her. He seemed far more fascinated with his briefcase, mumbling about all the work waiting for him. He said something about another trip to Europe before the end of summer.

Maybe he hadn't liked her kiss.

Hah! And he didn't like eggs in the morning, either.

Spring pulled herself together to listen to the morning service. Afterward, she visited the rest room to freshen her makeup before meeting Tyler. She applied her hairbrush with vigor, gritting her teeth, gaining a stack of backbone, she hoped. Why in the world couldn't she simply get over it?

She would, with God's help, she decided.

Gaining a little distance between her and Chad was the very thing she needed today. Besides that, she was eager to see her old friend. Tyler was a bit zany and would make her laugh. He'd take her mind off...other things.

She'd always found Tyler easy to talk with; he'd understood the closeness between her and Autumn. It would be fun to go out with him for the afternoon. He would remind her of home values.

She gave her hair a last flip, letting it fall straight to just past her shoulders. It had grown quite a bit since moving to New York; she supposed she could do with a good cut.

Home values. Her thoughts kept returning to this thing with Chad. She had to remind herself of God's values. That was where she'd draw strength.

The afternoon turned into evening. Toward nine, Spring let herself into the apartment.

"Have a good time?" Honor eagerly turned from her TV program to ask. "Why didn't you bring him back to say hello?"

"Yes," Spring answered with a chuckle. At Honor's age, she'd been curious about the whole world of dating. "I always enjoy Tyler's company. But he had an early flight tomorrow."

"Oh."

Was that disappointment in Honor's tone?

"What'd you do?"

"Oh, we walked up and down Broadway. Strolled around Rockefeller Center. Ate dinner. Talked of home and friends."

"Why is he in New York?"

Chad looked up at Honor's question, though he made a pretense of reading the newspaper. Had *he* wanted to ask that? Spring wondered.

"Did he just come to see you?" Honor persisted.

"I'm sure he was glad to see me," she said, shooting Chad a look. Chad promptly went back to his newspaper. "But no, he didn't come to New York just for that. He had business here."

"Oh...okay. Just as well." Honor returned to her TV show.

Now, what had her young friend meant by that? "Just as well?"

"Um, you know. Wouldn't want to disappoint him."

"Tyler's disappointment for anything—or not—

never rested on me,'' she explained carefully, wondering at Chad's silence.

Was he even interested in her answer? His attention seemed riveted on the paper.

"Well, I'm for bed, I think."

"G'night," he mumbled, folding the paper once more in front of his nose.

She wanted to cry. What was going on with Chad?

If he hadn't meant anything serious, if he only found her convenient for a little affection now and again, then she had to put a stop to it. She simply had to remain more...detached, she supposed. Not become so personally involved.

She had to move out entirely, or keep things businesslike. Keep her attention strictly on running the household. How she could do that when she had to face him every day, she didn't know.

That week, Honor doubled her ballet classes to make up for the ones she had missed during camp week. The instructor planned a recital for summer's end, and wanted all her students to practice daily.

Spring usually attended with her. Sometimes Leilani tagged along, hoping for a dropout so she could move up from the waiting list. Then one evening in the middle of the following week, she called to say it had happened. She'd been accepted. And what's more, the teacher was so impressed with Leilani's dedication, she was joining Honor's class.

Spring heard Leilani's squeal through the phone from across the room. Honor's was deafening.

A chuckle escaped. Chad strolled into the room, his brows raised in question. She explained.

He nearly groaned. "Does this mean we're in for it all the more?"

"I think it does." Then she laughed outright at his expression. "Teen mania eventually passes, though."

"Whatever happened to the notion that a man's home is his castle?"

"Um, are you sure you ever had one?"

"Did. Once. Not so sure anymore."

Yet, Spring didn't think him too put out. He had Lester come and move the dining room furniture aside to install a practice bar against the longest wall.

The girls practiced together daily. At Honor's urging, Spring sometimes went through the routine with them, although it was clear that both Honor and Leilani far outpaced her abilities. She didn't care. She enjoyed the exercise.

Since camp, Spring felt more grounded with her growing friendship with Dana, too. They chatted a moment or two almost every day now.

"Hey, Spring," Dana said by way of greeting toward the end of the week. "I need your help on a new program for our teens."

"Oh? What kind of program?"

"Well…it won't appeal to all of 'em. That's why I'm hoping you can help."

"Just spit it out, Dana."

"Okay. Here's the deal. I want to develop a visiting program with our teens for our older members. Something on a regular basis. Especially to visit the shut-ins. Some of our kids have grown up with grandparents in the home. They know what aging and the three generational family is all about. But many of them don't. Some of 'em don't have a close older relative at all. These are the ones I want to reach."

"Where do I come in?" Spring asked.

"Well, you told me about growing up with an older uncle. That's great training. You can teach these kids what to expect, let them know how to make friends across an age gap. I'm thinking of making this program into a regular thing. What do you think?"

"Honor was really impressed with Mrs. Pine and Mr. Steward when they came to talk with us a couple of months back."

"Yeah, I know," Dana said. "I've been thinking about that. That's what started this whole idea. It would teach the kids another way to serve the Lord by serving others. So how about it?"

To serve... The term sparkled into life, recalling Spring's earlier questions about it. Hadn't the Scriptures talked about Jesus as a servant? She tried to recall the one, then decided she'd have to look it up later.

"I'd like that, Dana," she said, feeling decisive. "I think I could really get into it."

They made arrangements to meet and discuss their first steps toward developing their goals.

This might be the thing to help her put some emotional distance between herself and Chad, Spring mused. If she had another focus, it would give her an extra buffer against her own runaway emotions; anyway, it would take up a chunk of time.

She didn't see why this would even matter to the others. Honor had her growing circle of teens, and besides work, Chad had an established social circle of his own—one in which she didn't fit. So while she worked to find a job in design, this project could fill her time off.

But she hadn't counted on Chad springing the need for a trip to Virginia.

"I talked with the estate manager today," he said over dinner. "She says she's been by the house and checked on it recently. Everything's in pretty good order, except some of the wood roof shakes need replacing. She thinks we should have it inspected, too. I thought we'd take a long weekend and run down."

Honor didn't answer immediately, pushing her salad around in her bowl. "When?"

"Next week."

"I don't want to miss any more ballet classes, Chad." She didn't look up. "We have a recital in August. I want to be ready."

"C'mon, Honor, you'll do fine." He frowned

slightly, then pressed it. "Besides, don't you want to see a few of your Virginia friends? Who's that girl you sometimes get mail from? Courtney? And I should pick up some things, check out some others. There's been stuff you've mentioned wanting from there, too."

"I s'pose," Honor agreed, though she didn't attempt to hide her reluctance. Her heart wasn't in it.

Chad laid a hand on her arm, letting his expression soften. Her hair fell in loose braids against her shoulders, a style she'd taken to wearing at camp. He brushed the tail of one, his affection for his sister at an all-time high.

"We don't have to, ah…sort Dad's things just yet, honey. But we are going to have to do it one day soon. And make a few decisions about the house. We've let the task slide."

"I s'pose," she said again. Brown eyes gleamed with apprehension. "It's just that I'm afraid I'll… miss Mom and Dad so much. Living here, it's easier."

"Yeah… Yeah."

He let a moment go by.

"It's a tough one, I'll grant you that." He patted her arm, then tugged on the braid. He let a smile spread. "But you've got me now, Honor Suzanne. We Alexanders are a team, aren't we? We can face it together."

"Will you come with me, Spring?"

Spring looked up from her own salad. "Oh,

sweetie, I think this should be just you and Chad. You two are family.''

"Yes, but you—you're...'' Honor cast a glance toward Chad, then bit her lip.

"I wish you would, Spring.''

Chad's simple request came with a deeper one conveyed by his gaze. A slight nod told her he really wanted her to accept.

"We already owe you a lot of time, I know, but this would really help.''

Spring drew a deep breath, then turned to Honor. She might as well try to deny Autumn the right to breathe, she'd have just about as much chance of saying no. This child needed her.

"Okay, I'll trade you. I'll go with you to Virginia. We'll take care of whatever you need, I'll help with it. But will you come along with this new program Dana and I are working on?''

"What's that?'' Honor asked. Her expression grew a bit suspicious, but brightened. "It isn't anything dumb, is it?''

"Not a bit. It's a people thing, an idea to bring our church members into more of a family. We especially need the teens. In fact, I think you might very well be the one to help spearhead it. Maybe you, Leilani and Dillon.'' Spring threw in the boy she knew Honor had a mild crush on, thinking herself brilliant to remember him. "And we'd be serving the Lord.''

"All right, I guess. But I can't promise much.''

"Good,'' Chad said. "That's settled. We'll drive

down Friday and come back Tuesday. Is that all right with you?''

"Sure,'' Spring answered. She thought it time to change the subject. "By the way, Honor, the other day while waiting for you to finish your class, I met a young woman who designs theater costumes. Oh, she doesn't do anything big. Like me, she's just getting started. But she has a connection, someone who's backing her. She hopes to establish a line soon. She invited me to come see her collection sometime.''

"Sounds fun,'' Honor agreed.

"Yeah, doesn't it? And from the clothes she had on, I'd say she likes splash and bright colors. I asked where she found her fabrics. She said she'd give me names and things. Her sponsor gets her a huge discount. Nice to have such connections, hmm? That's what I need, I think. Someone who can put me in touch with the right people. I'd love some decent appointments.''

Chad set his coffee cup down. Connections. Someone who could give her an in.

Old suspicions wormed up his spine. Did she— *had* she—known of his tie with Jonathan Feathers? Jonathan and Libby were an easy touch when it came to sponsoring the arts. They often mixed with the creative people. Why shouldn't he know of someone connected to Spring's field?

Had Spring thought of that? Was she hoping for an introduction?

Chapter Sixteen

The home that Chad and Honor had grown up in appeared on the horizon like a movie fantasy. Set atop a hill in rolling countryside, the two-story red-brick structure looked as though it had been there since the founding of the states. Trees and white fences surrounded it like a picture frame. Spring thought it all worthy of the most idealistic of novels.

"Well, I'm impressed," Spring murmured. She tried to keep her mouth from dropping open. Nothing had prepared her. Chad carried no southern accent, and Honor's was minimal. But this estate cried wealth. Old money. "You didn't tell me you had your own plantation."

Honor sat forward in her seat, her anxiety turning to eagerness as they pulled into the long drive.

"Not really," Chad answered. "Our roots here are only one generation deep. Dad bought this place to entertain and impress his business connections. We did a lot of that when I was a kid. We didn't grow anything here, or produce much of anything.''

"Dad kept horses," Honor put in. "My mom loved to ride. But now the pastures are leased out. See?'' She pointed to five horses standing in the shade of a tree clump. ''This front pasture is ours, but those belong to our neighbors.''

"You must miss all this terribly,'' Spring said, glancing first at Chad, then Honor. New York seemed a different world entirely.

Then she could have bit her tongue. Honor's eyes told too much of her feelings, and she didn't answer.

Chad opened his mouth to speak, then apparently changed his mind. He simply parked the car where the drive circled in front of the house. Three wide steps led to a tall, dark-red paneled door. Narrow side windows flanked it.

Chad unlocked the door, then stepped back to let his sister enter. Spring dawdled in getting her bag from the trunk, thinking that Honor and Chad might need a few moments alone with their family home and memories. But he turned and beckoned her through.

Flipping light switches, Chad made a wordless sound of satisfaction when he saw the hall light come on.

''Not all the circuit breakers are switched full time. Mr. Jamison is supposed to make rounds at least once a week to check on things. I gave instructions for the electricity, but I saw no reason to have the phones turned on for only a weekend, Honor, so you'll have to make your calls with my cell phone.''

Honor didn't answer. Instead, she dropped her overnight case in the hall and ran to a room in the rear. After a moment, she returned carrying a giant brown teddy bear, his fur ragged. He filled her arms.

''My Theodore Bear. I've had him since I was born. I've missed him.''

Spring glanced around her, while Chad continued to check things out.

Huge rooms opened off the front-to-back center hall, which was lined with old paintings and mirrors. Honor led her from one to another with the excitement of a proud home owner. While each was filled with antique furniture, the small study desk had an old computer and both parlors also held comfortable modern couches.

In the smaller parlor, a large-screen television sat between windows that looked out on a bricked terrace. Floor-to-ceiling shelves flanked the fireplace; a stereo system was tucked away between hardbound books there. One low shelf carried several stuffed animals, games and children's books.

The room smelled musty, yet Spring knew instantly that this was where the family had gathered most. It carried a casual lived-in look.

They ended in the kitchen. It was the one room that had been totally remodeled to accommodate modern appliances. Surprisingly, it was rather small.

"Long ago, this was a servant's room," Honor explained. "Before, when kitchens were a separate building."

Chad turned on the water in the sink. The pressure seemed fine.

"All right. Groceries next," Chad said as he headed back outside to the car. They'd grabbed burgers and fries on the outer edge of Arlington for supper. Then they'd stopped at a grocery store to purchase enough food to see them through the weekend. "I'm ready for a snack."

"Me, too. But first I'll show Spring my room," Honor said eagerly. Spring followed the girl up the narrow back stairway off the kitchen.

They wandered through the upper floor, while Spring made appropriate comments and swooned over the guest room in which she would sleep. The house was a living museum, she mused as they returned to the first floor by way of the front hall staircase. Not as huge as many of the old Virginia mansions, but lovely and inviting, just the same. She felt as though she'd stepped back in time.

"How could you not have known much about the war between the states in the middle of all this?" she asked Honor as they reached the kitchen again.

Spring watched Chad empty the last grocery bag, sticking cartons of milk and orange juice into the old refrigerator.

"Well, I guess it just didn't come together for me

before we began to really study it," Honor replied. "What did you get to munch on, Chad?"

"Chips and cheese dip," he said, grinning at Spring. He watched her give an exaggerated sigh. She'd insisted on adding fruit to their grocery basket—the healthy choice, she'd said. "Let's watch the news and relax a while."

He grabbed three soft drinks, adding them to the tray he'd already filled with his choices, then led the way into the small parlor. Spring sat in the sofa corner, curling her legs beneath her. Chad placed the tray on a large square coffee table and sat down in the overstuffed chair opposite.

Honor found the remote control and punched the on switch. Nothing happened.

"Oh-oh. Won't come on."

"It may if you plug it in," Chad instructed with a dry tone.

"All right, smarty-pants." Honor made a face at him, then stooped to find the cord. "Didn't think."

"Everything's been unplugged and turned off while we weren't here," Chad said by way of explanation. "Except for a light in the kitchen and one in the front, so that occasional lights could be timed to turn on at night to keep intruders at bay."

"Your parents must have done a lot of work here to keep the wiring up to code," Spring murmured.

"Yes, they certainly did." Chad slid down more comfortably in his chair. "Dad tried hard to keep the old alive along with the new, though. He loved this place. I had so much local history shoved at me along with my morning cereal that I just tuned out.''

"Me, too, I guess," Honor said. "Boring."

"I must have been a real disappointment to Dad. I was more interested in the normal things kids usually are—school, girls, basketball, girls, cars, girls..."

"Yeah," Honor agreed, poking her brother in the ribs. "Dad said you were a real high school stud, Chad. Too bad you don't have any girlfriends left in Virginia. You could call one. What did you do to lose 'em all?"

"Oh, I have a name or two I could still call if I wanted, brat. I just like dating women where I live."

Spring laced her fingers together. She thought Chad's statement a true reflection of his feelings. He didn't date anyone with any serious intent, she'd decided. Why should she take any of his flirtations personally? She was merely one of many.

"That reminds me," Honor said. "I want to call a couple of people. Gimme your phone."

Honor held out her open palm. Chad grunted, then handed over the small pocket phone.

"We've lost her now," he complained. "She won't come up for air till midnight."

"She's missed her home here—it's natural for her to want to talk to her friends."

"Yeah. I know." He took a swallow of his cola, then raised a brow. "Want to go for a walk outside? I could use the exercise after that long drive."

"Sure. It's really beautiful countryside." She rose, tugging her shirt down over her waist. "It's getting cool. I'll just get long sleeves."

They left the house through the kitchen door. Chad led her down a back drive toward an old building that he described as a one-time smokehouse. A detached garage, down a back slope, had once been the carriage house, he explained. "It has an apartment above it. Been thinking of sprucing it up. It might be just the enticement for a good full-time caretaker.

"If it were up to me, I'd sell this place," he added, letting a sigh escape.

He took her elbow and guided their steps around the smokehouse to a path that led along the rail fence. Two sleek mares of similar color lifted their heads to stare at them curiously.

"But I don't think Honor is anywhere near such a thought," he continued. "I've been talking with Walter Peebles. Dad left the estate to both of us, but if she wants the house after she comes of age, I want to hold it for her."

"That's wonderfully generous of you, Chad," she said. "But don't you miss this place as much as she does?"

"I should, I suppose. But no, not really. I like living in New York. That's where my life is, where the hub of my practice is. If I should ever decide to buy a house, I'd find one in Rockland County, Long

Island or White Plains. Somewhere close enough for daily commute.''

He smiled suddenly, the curves of his mouth giving his cheeks that slashing fold Spring liked. ''Besides, my dad's folks were really Yankees. Their history is in New England, so we're interlopers here.''

They strolled until the path gave out, then followed the fence line through the uncut grass until they'd reached a dirt road.

In the quiet, birds called across the dusk and frogs sounded deep croaks from a wide pond. Peace descended with the evening sun.

''This road divides us from our south neighbor,'' Chad said. They climbed through the fence, and then he jumped the weed-choked ditch to the road. Recent rain had filled it. He turned, taking her hand to help her do the same.

Sliding his hand to grip her elbow, he gave a small yank.

She stumbled forward, her feet barely clearing the weeds, against him. He caught her as though it were something he'd rehearsed. His arms circled and tightened, pulling her to his chest.

Her breath quickened as she raised her gaze to meet one of sparkling, teasing mirth. He bent his head, his mouth only inches from hers.

A rush of doubt assailed her as her heart picked up its beat. She'd shared kisses twice with this man. Both times had left her a muddled, shaking mess. She couldn't let this go on; Chad would have all of her without giving anything of himself in return, if she wasn't careful.

And, oh! It would be so easy to give in—loving him as she did.

The thought of loving him didn't startle her at all. She'd fallen in love with Chad Alexander from almost that first night—though she just this moment realized that truth. He'd been so grave and suspicious, but then when he did smile, she'd been knocked out.

Her breath came from a long way down. She hadn't a real prayer with Chad. He might want to pursue their mutual attraction, but he wasn't ready for any kind of commitment. Certainly not marriage. Besides, he wanted a sophisticated New York woman. She'd never be that.

No, she'd never be a Big Apple sophisticate, but she knew how to be herself. She had ambitions of her own. Ones that could very well take her somewhere; but for now she was here, with Chad.

She lifted her chin and smiled. Slowly. Anticipating his kiss...

"Chaaadd..." From a distance, they heard Honor's faint call. "Spriinnng."

Chad groaned. Why now?

Spring turned toward the sound. "Maybe something's wrong. We'd better hurry."

"I don't think it's anything serious." He seemed reluctant to let her go, resting his forehead against hers. "She'd ring the cowbell if it was."

Nevertheless, he let her go. They quickened their return.

"It's Anne Martin from your firm," Honor said, as soon as they came through the door. "She wants you to call her right back."

Chad threw Spring an apologetic glance, then took the phone Honor handed him. "I'm surprised she could wedge her call in," he teased.

"Well, if you'd get me one of my own, we wouldn't have to share," Honor shot back with a grimace. "I haven't even called Courtney yet."

"Nothing spoiled about her, is there?" he muttered so that only Spring could hear.

"She's merely reflecting her age and how the other kids are, Chad. Don't be too hard on her. She'll outgrow this stage."

He nodded, and let his irritation slide away. His sister was usually an unselfish child.

He took the phone into his father's study. Sitting in the old leather executive chair, worn with his father's shape, he leaned back, propping his feet on the desk corner.

"You missed all the fun," Anne said as soon as he reached her.

"What? Nothing disastrous, I hope."

"Well, only this side of it. Hopping, to say the least. Hasn't Jonathan reached you?"

"Uh-uh. What's up?"

"The brothers—Ken and Lawrence—announced

their retirement from the firm today. Effective September first.''

"No lie!" His feet hit the floor as he sat forward.

"Yeah. Didn't you know about it?"

"Not this. Not this soon. Ken was due—he'd been downsizing his load all year—but Jonathan said he wouldn't go before the end of the year. Both of them? Why now?"

"They said they're moving to Florida. Said they might set up a little practice down there, but mostly they just wanted to go deep-sea fishing."

"Wow! What did Jonathan say?"

"I can't believe he hasn't reached you yet."

"Couldn't get through, I suppose." At his sister's insistence, he'd turned off his car phone during the drive down. She was becoming more cunning about getting her share of his time. "Honor's had my phone. So what else?"

"Not a lot significant. The usual. Jonathan mentioned their valuable contributions over the years, etcetera. Said we'd go through some reorganization, but not to worry, we'd be taking on some new people. Chad...how're my chances?"

He sucked in a deep breath, his thoughts dashing from one point to the other of this latest event.

"Very good, Anne. Excellent, in fact. Look, I need to talk with Jonathan. I'll be in touch."

He hung up, then punched in the number for Jonathan's home. Nothing in their last partner meeting had indicated that both brothers were going out at the same time.

"Sorry, Chad, it came up out of the blue," Jonathan said immediately when they connected. "Wasn't fair to you, the way things fell out. But Ken was adamant about not putting off his announcement. Something personal, no doubt. But the boys seemed to make up their minds to leave together. Puts us in a bind, really. Sorry to cut your weekend short, but I need you back here ASAP. We've called a meeting for eight o'clock Monday morning."

"Right. I'll be there."

He hung up. He sat a moment to let his thoughts settle. He hated to disappoint his sister. In spite of her sadness, she'd been so joyous to be back here. He thought it good for her to have time to deal more fully with her grief. And they still hadn't touched sorting out his dad's things. There were boxes stored in one upstairs closet that had been his mother's, too. As long as Dad was alive, he hadn't felt any need to go through them. He should at least look through them.

He hadn't given any thought to how Honor and his dad had coped with Sandra's things. He knew there were a few pieces of jewelry Honor had inherited, now tucked away for when she came of age. He had a few pieces of his own mother's in a safety deposit box.

Shoving his hands deep in his pockets, he headed

to rejoin the women. Honor wasn't going to take the change in plans lightly. He set himself to weather a storm of emotion.

Lord, help me to make wise decisions for my sister. Send my thoughts along the right path.

Chapter Seventeen

In the end, Chad drove with Spring and Honor early on Saturday into Dulles Airport, where he caught a shuttle flight to New York. He'd closed his phone call with Jonathan, agreeing to meet on Sunday afternoon to prepare for Monday morning.

He hated leaving Honor and Spring behind, but he'd caved in when Honor pitched a contrary fit about losing the promised weekend at home. As well, he left with grave doubts about Spring driving in to the city.

"I'm a competent driver, Chad," she assured him as he handed her the car keys. Her fingers closed around them, still warm from his palm. Then his hand wrapped around hers while he studied her with an unusual concentration.

"Wish I didn't have to leave. I'd hoped..." Disappointment laced his words, he knew. He let his hand drop and raked it through his hair. "Don't let Honor rule the weekend, hear? And lock all your doors."

"It will be all right, Chad. We can take care of ourselves. We'll be safe."

He nodded. "And take it easy coming in to the city."

"You sound like Dad, you know that?" Honor said as she impulsively kissed his cheek. "We aren't helpless without you. Or dummies. Spring and I can manage perfectly well."

"Uh-huh." His sister was only half-teasing. Chad narrowed his eyes at her and bit back a snappy retort. A few months back he hadn't worried about anyone but himself and now he felt plagued with concerns about two young females.

"I'll drive carefully," Spring said. "Promise."

"Even good drivers have trouble coping with city traffic in the Big Apple, Spring."

"True," she agreed, letting him see the amusement that hovered just beneath her placating words. "I can time it so we'll come in to the city at three in the morning. Would that ease your worries?"

"Don't be pert!" he popped back, trying to hide his own grin. But a mixture of emotions warred in his chest.

"Now admit it," Honor said, rolling her eyes. "That sounded just like Dad."

"Don't be sassy, either," he shot at Honor, then recalled that his father had used that expression with great fondness. *Pert and sass, that's what your mother is full of—pert and sass...*

Oh, Lord! He was becoming his father!

"Daddy used to call me Miss Pert sometimes," Honor remarked, cementing Chad's sudden revelation.

Spring's gaze, full of curiosity and empathy, sliced through his thoughts. Perhaps he was more like his dad than he knew, but he didn't feel a bit fatherly about this one female in his household with blue-green eyes that looked right through him. Who sometimes saw the empty state of his heart.

He'd be wise to close off that access, he thought for the millionth time. Only he thought it just might be too late. *Knew* it was too late. The wonder was that he hadn't been aware his heart had become empty until Spring and his sister came along to fill it.

He swallowed hard. Behind him, the airline gave out the last boarding call.

"Just take it easy, okay? Don't challenge any cab drivers."

"All right."

Spring smiled with the sweetness he'd come to expect, and he thought his heart would overflow. He'd never felt so confused over a woman before, never had to face down a tenderness while wanting so badly to take her off somewhere and forget the world existed.

What had happened to his love of his work? To

his dedication to his firm, his contentment with the people he served there? Sure it took a lot of time. A mountain of it. And he'd never minded giving it before. But he'd never before owned a personal life, either.

"I'll slow to a creep the moment we hit traffic," Spring added as a last teasing reassurance.

"Gotta go." He gave a harried chuckle, and waved as he got on the plane. "Call me when you leave. And again when you reach the city."

Spring calmly waved back at him.

When Spring drove carefully into the city on Monday night, she and Honor were a day earlier than scheduled. Much to her surprise, Honor had been ready to return to the city.

They found Chad and a white-haired man seated at the dining table, stacks of papers spread before them, with dirty glasses, coffee cups and an empty pizza box pushed to one side. Tired lines etched their eyes. Both had discarded suit jackets and ties.

Both men looked up as she and Honor entered the apartment.

Chad blinked, then glanced at his watch. "What the—? It's eleven o'clock. Why now?" He rose and came toward them. "I thought you weren't coming in till tomorrow?"

"We were ready to be home," Spring said simply. She smiled toward the older man, who stared at her and Honor with bright curiosity. "Sorry to interrupt."

After hours in the car, she felt grungy and in need of a shower. Her shorts were crumpled, and her hair, in short braids so it would be out of her eyes, sprouted stubby ends. There could have been a better time to meet Chad's boss, she silently moaned.

"Jonathan, I'd like you to meet my sister, Honor Suzanne, and our friend, Spring Barbour. You've heard me speak of them, of course."

She and Honor murmured the appropriate greetings.

"You didn't call," Chad accused, then added suspiciously, "Where's the car?"

"What if I told you we, um, got crunched in a five-car pile up and sat for three hours waiting till the cops sorted us out and the car had to be towed?" Honor said, glancing up at her brother with mock shame.

"Watch it, brat, or I might tow *you*," Chad replied.

"You don't believe that?" his sister asked a little too demurely. "I'm dying of thirst, doesn't that tell you anything?"

"Not a jot." Behind him, he heard Jonathan chuckle. He raised questioning brows at Spring.

"Um, Lester promised to park it for us," Spring said. She wouldn't admit to feeling so wrung-out over the harrowing experience of city traffic that she couldn't bring herself to drive it one last half-block to the garage. "But we left him unloading all the stuff Honor wanted to bring."

Chad pursed his mouth. "Lester? He's usually off duty by now."

"We called him ahead of time," Honor put in. Spring shot her an exasperated glare, to which she mumbled, "Sorry."

"You called Lester but not me?" Chad challenged.

"Weelll…" Honor drew out the word. "You did say you were really, really busy. We didn't want you to have a tizzy."

"See what I have to put up with at home, Jonathan?" Chad complained loudly. "A brat and a rebel."

Jonathan, still chuckling, turned to pick up his coat and tie, then rose to walk toward them with a pleasant smile. "We have, indeed, been very busy, young lady. But we'll call it a night, Chad."

"Sorry, Jonathan," Chad muttered, serious once more. "That leaves a heavy day for tomorrow."

"Not to fret. We'll tackle it all in due time. Your family is home now. But I think we've made good strides, Chad. The firm may take a dip until we can reorganize without the Sanders brothers, but we'll come around."

"Good. At least we're ready for tomorrow's early meeting. I suppose it will take the whole morning." He frowned. "I'd better have Anne…hmm, I'll need to hire someone new to take Anne's place now that she's moving up, won't I?'' He ran a hand against the back of his neck. ''This week will be quite a ride, I'm sure.''

''Yes, yes, I suspect so,'' Jonathan replied. ''I plan to remain in the city the rest of this week, do a little extra courting of clients, you might say.'' He sighed. ''My Libby doesn't like it when I stay in the city without her. She complains I don't eat properly or get enough rest. She's threatened to stay with me to make sure I behave.''

''I'll ring for a taxi,'' Chad said, reaching for his cell phone, which was lying on the dining room table.

''I'll do that,'' Spring insisted. ''While you fellows gather up your work. Are you sure you wouldn't like something to eat before you go?'' she asked Jonathan.

''Thank you, my dear, that's very kind of you to offer.'' The older man's eyes lit with gratitude. ''But no.... Perhaps you, Honor Suzanne, and Chad will join Libby and me for dinner soon. We love the company of young people.''

''We'd be delighted,'' Spring answered. ''I do hope you and Chad don't have to put in too many long hours this week. But if you're staying in the city to work long days, anyway, you must plan to have dinner with us a time or two. It will be so much easier and more comfortable for you than eating out each time.''

"My, my, you are a rare jewel. Are you interested in the law perhaps? Or office support?"

"Sorry, sir, not really. I have other directions to follow."

"Ah…"

"I'll just see you down, Jonathan," Chad said.

It seemed to take Chad a long time to return. Spring dawdled, making hot chocolate, while Honor went to bed. He finally followed Lester up with the dozen boxes Honor had brought home. He helped Lester pile them in the front hall, tipped him generously, then closed and locked the door.

"Want some?" Spring said, handing him a full cup.

"Yeah, sure. Thanks."

Spring carried hers into the living room and curled up in the big chair. She sipped slowly. Chad drank from his cup, then sprawled on the couch, his head tipped back, his eyes closed. Was he worried about the law firm? Or his place there?

She watched him, wishing to soothe away his exhaustion but not daring to move an inch closer. If she got within touching distance…

She remained still. They both needed rest and sleep. Letting themselves unwind without interference seemed the best course of action.

Beneath half-closed lids, he locked into her gaze. "Glad you're safely home," he murmured.

He seemed more than usually thoughtful. "Mmm…"

"Jonathan mentioned having Libby call you."

"That's sweet of him."

"You impressed him."

"Oh?" It didn't seem to Spring there had been enough time or interchange to impress anyone. "How so?"

"You don't seem intimidated by anything."

She couldn't tell him that loving him scared her to her back teeth. Or face the truth of it, as she had been doing for the last few days. Or the idea of telling him at all, when she wasn't sure he'd want that love. But she only said, "Why should I be?"

"No reason. Now I think I'll say good-night. These next few weeks will be a bear. Can't say what hours I'll be home."

She simply nodded, and remained seated as she listened to his door close.

True to his statement, Chad was home little over the next few days. He left the apartment early and came home late. The weekend came and went with only a lightening of the load on Sunday. Chad attended church with them, but excused himself to work at his desk after they returned home.

On Tuesday, Spring called Gerald Designs again, where she'd left a few sketches for consideration. She made a couple of other calls while waiting for Honor to finish her ballet class, including to the New York Branch of the LaSalle School of Design. But the young woman she'd talked with hadn't known much about the decisions of student acceptance. She'd receive a notice by the end of the month if she was on the list, the woman had said.

On Wednesday, a flat, well-padded and insured package came from Autumn. In it Spring found wedding pictures; she picked up the first of the professionally posed ones and studied it. Her sister, beautiful and glowing with confidence, and Brent, smiling broadly, stared back at her. Their faces shone with so much love, it made her cry.

The second was of Autumn and her. The next half-dozen were snapshots of the entire wedding party: Spring and Honor; Timmy—Brent's son—with cake on his face; Brent's family; friends.

At the bottom of the package were two watercolor paintings. One was of the church Autumn and Brent loved so much, and the second, meant for Honor, was of a small boy flying a kite.

Spring felt a sudden wave of homesickness. She instantly picked up the phone and spent a long hour talking with her sister. It wasn't hard to tell that her sister was the happiest she'd ever been. Autumn was more free of the fears she'd had than Spring had ever known her sister to be.

"It's truly a release," Autumn told her. "I still won't put myself in a mob of people deliberately, but that feeling of something choking me, that clamping of my heart so tightly that the blood can't flow when I find myself in even a reasonable crowd…is all gone. My faith in God has given me the courage I never thought I had. And Timmy and I have the best time shopping at the grocery store together. In the middle of the day!"

Spring laughed. Yes, her sister's happiness could be no less that God's blessing. Spring hung up, owning to the tiniest bit of envy of her sister.

About four on Thursday afternoon, Chad called. "What's going on tonight?" he asked without more than a hello.

"What do you mean? Not much, actually. Why?"

"Um, I want to bring Jonathan home. We're both dog tired of the office and need a break, but we have to draft something for a client by tomorrow." He hesitated for a breath. "And Anne Martin."

"Sure. Of course." It was his apartment. He could bring home whomever he pleased.

"I was wondering…if you could make dinner."

He'd never asked this kind of thing from her. Yet she found she didn't really mind. Why should she object? "Any requests?"

"Whatever you can manage on short notice will be just fine."

The grateful relief in his voice was palpable.

"About seven?"

"Not a problem."

In her room, Spring folded up the fabric she'd been sewing, a Noah's ark costume she'd promised to the church nursery. She had plenty of time to run out to find fresh fruit, vegetables and a flank steak that she could marinate, broil and slice into thin strips.

She asked Honor to set the table. They worked in tandem, listening to one of Honor's CDs. She timed the dinner to be served at seven-thirty, giving the partners plenty of time to arrive.

And Anne Martin. She couldn't forget Anne. Anne had been made an associate on the fast track to becoming a partner, Chad had told her not long ago.

Anne was a whirlwind at corporate law; Chad missed her as his personal assistant. They had hired a new one, but he already knew the woman wasn't nearly as sharp as Anne.

They had two new people on board, so his work should slow down very soon, he'd added. One of them would work with Anne. And they were considering a merger with another small firm, one that would fill out their areas of expertise. Chad felt in favor of it. He and Jonathan were still discussing the matter, he'd told Spring.

Just before seven, Spring showered and changed into her favorite summer dress, the turquoise knit that brought out the blue-green of her eyes. She complemented it with matching enameled earrings that dangled against her neck.

"What a lovely table, my dear," Jonathan said later. "It is kind of you to ask us, but you needn't have gone to so much trouble. Chad and I were extremely tired of office walls. Anne never complains—'' he nodded in her direction ''—but she must hate them as much as we do by now after the past weeks. Need to take care of these clients, though. Midsize-hotel people wanting to broaden their sites in Europe.''

''We're not troubled, Jonathan,'' Spring answered. ''Cooking is one of my hobbies. It's creative, and for some reason all kinds of designs suggest themselves to me while I'm cooking. I've been known to run from the kitchen to the drawing board with my face smeared with flour or cookie dough.''

Jonathan chuckled.

''If it were me, I'd have the whole bag of flour all over the kitchen,'' Anne said and laughed. ''And it wouldn't be a pretty sight. I don't cook.''

Chad smiled, too, but it seemed to Spring that his mind was elsewhere.

When dinner was over, Jonathan insisted on helping to clear the table. That done, Spring served coffee, while the men and Anne got out their briefcases. Honor retreated to the living room to watch a movie. After she'd cleaned the kitchen, Spring fetched the costume she was working on, quietly sitting with Honor while she completed a little handwork.

They worked till almost one in the morning. Then Honor went to bed; Spring remained awake, making sure the three had whatever they might need.

''This should do it,'' Jonathan finally said as he shuffled a sheaf of papers together. ''If we keep these people happy now, we can count on keeping them in the future.''

Spring said good-night, leaving Chad to see the guests to the door. She carried the dirty cups and water glasses into the kitchen, while Chad rode down the elevator with them, making sure each had a taxi.

"Here's the mail," Chad said a few minutes later, coming back into the apartment. "It came late today, I guess. Something here for you."

"There wasn't anything in our box when I checked," she murmured, surprised. Accepting the long brown envelope, she almost put it aside to finish loading the dishwasher.

Then the return address caught her eye—the LaSalle School of Design. The one she'd given up on ever granting her a place. She held the envelope a moment, not breathing. Then she tore it open.

It was a letter of acceptance. "Oh! Oh! *Oh!*"

"What is it?" Chad asked.

"I—I've been accepted in the LaSalle School of Design's basic program. They're accepting only a few students this year…. Oh, I can't believe it. They have an opening in their school in *Paris!* Oh, Chad…Paris. They say I can have a place there. Imagine…"

"Congratulations, Spring. It's what you've wanted all along, isn't it?"

"Only everything I've ever dreamed."

"I'm very pleased for you. Um, how soon will we lose you?"

All the excitement drained out of her.

If she were to accept, she'd have to leave within two weeks. Leave Honor before her dance recital. Leave Honor when she'd promised to be around for the girl's birthday in September. Leave Dana with unfinished costumes for her Noah's ark play. Leave before she could help with the church gathering of seniors and teens. Leave Chad without telling him how much she loved him. Leave, with no promise of seeing him tomorrow. Or the next day.

Leave Chad... Live in Paris without him....

Chapter Eighteen

Mixed emotions stirred Spring awake the next morning. A funny sadness combined with a weighted anticipation. She lay for a moment, trying to make heads or tails of it before getting up. She couldn't recall the last time she hadn't been in charge of her feelings. Yet lately, they'd run wild without ever looking back to see if she followed.

The mid-morning sun slanting through her window told her she'd slept late. The quiet around her indicated that Honor was still in bed. Honor would have to be up within an hour for ballet class. Finally, Spring pushed herself out of bed and dressed.

Chad had left her a note in the kitchen. She was to take the day to do whatever she wanted for herself. Not to bother with dinner tonight. He and Honor could take care of themselves.

Did that mean he wanted to begin putting distance between her and Honor?

She lay the note aside and made herself a cup of tea. Then she called Autumn from the kitchen phone, keeping her voice low while telling her sister of the newest development in her life. Autumn asked lots of enthusiastic questions, many for which Spring didn't have answers. She tried to show her elation over her good fortune.

Oh, yeah, she tried.

At least, she *should* feel that kind of glow, she told herself. She was going to Paris to study, after all. What aspiring fashion designer wouldn't want to study there? It was what she'd always dreamed of doing.

Only, why didn't she feel happy?

Autumn kindly didn't remark on Spring's lack of high spirits. Hanging up, Spring felt like a fraud. She didn't understand her own muddled emotions, or her downright disinclination to rush around packing her bags.

The phone rang. Leilani greeted her before asking for Honor.

"Just a minute," Spring said, and hid her disappointment that it wasn't Chad. What was he doing today? How were the plans to merge with the other firm coming along?

A few minutes later, Honor rumbled into the kitchen, still tousled from sleep, complaining she wouldn't have time for breakfast, and asking why

Spring had let her sleep so late? And was it all right for her and Leilani to spend the afternoon in the extra practice hall, next to where the class was held?

The ballet recital was growing closer, and the girls were more excited with each class.

"What's wrong with your alarm?" Spring asked her.

A fleeting look of dawning guilt crossed Honor's face, and Spring laughed.

"Guess I shoulda set it," Honor admitted. "Got out of the habit when school was out. You're usually already up, anyway. Are you coming into class today? Please say yes. I want you to check out how I stand in the line."

"I'm sure Mrs. Greenleaf will change you if you aren't doing well where you are."

"But I trust you, Spring."

"All right. I'll stay to observe."

They were about to leave the apartment, when Anne Martin called. "I wanted to thank you again for your hospitality last night, Spring," she said. "You went to a lot of extra work."

"Actually, it wasn't a lot of bother, Anne." The compliment pleased her. "I really do like to cook. Besides, it's my job, in a way. Chad pays me to keep his home tidy and to be a companion for Honor. Honor and I usually prepare meals together. Including two extra was rather fun."

"Well, if you ever get tired of working there, please let me know. I'd hire you in a minute. But then, Chad explains that you're really a dress designer in disguise. Just taking a break from your real goals to do a temporary favor for them as Honor's friend.''

A warm feeling flowed around Spring's heart. Chad hadn't taken her for granted at all. It explained a lot. She liked the fact that he now understood Honor's need for her friendship, and that he thought of her as an equal in the household.

"Psst." Already at the apartment door to leave, Honor beckoned and mouthed, *Hurry. Gotta go.*

Spring held up a finger, indicating that she'd be there shortly.

"That's a good description of it, I guess," she said into the phone. "Although I still pursue my own interests."

"So I hear. You must be so excited about the offer to study in Paris."

"Yes, I am." Surprise gave her pause. She turned away from Honor's nagging stare. "My goodness! Chad was certainly quick to tell you about it. I can't imagine you'd be interested."

"Oh, he was on the phone for an hour one day last week before he got frustrated and went to Jonathan. Jonathan made very short work of the matter, I guess."

"I don't understand. How does Jonathan Feathers enter into this?" And she'd received the news only last night, after everyone had gone. Why would people in Chad's office know of her plans?

"Didn't you realize? That LaSalle school is on the list of investments in the arts that he and Libby Feathers support. Libby's on their board of directors. Libby loves to help struggling artists and writers and theater people. Design is a part of that. The Feathers put their money where their mouths are. Jonathan knew right away whom to talk to about your entry. I'm only surprised Libby hasn't asked to meet you yet."

"Spring, we'll be late," Honor said again.

"The opportunity hasn't come up," Spring said into the phone. "I'm sorry, Anne, but Honor is due for her ballet class. I must go."

"Oh, sorry. I won't keep you."

Spring gave a pleasant goodbye, and she and Honor rushed out. They reached the class just as the warm-up exercises began. True to her promise, Spring sat along the side with another woman, watching the practice with only half her attention.

She had time to think. To feel the shock set in as realization and hurt swirled in her head. Chad had arranged for her offer. At that particular school. In Paris.

He *wanted* her to leave. He'd made arrangements to send her far away.

Granted, LaSalle School had a good reputation and carried a lovely scholarship, something she hadn't dreamed of gaining. Had he arranged that, too? She hadn't even thought of it, wanting only acceptance. She'd been willing to pay the high tuition fees.

Did Chad want her out of Honor's life, then? Out of his? Had their convenient exchange become a liability for him in some way? Was she somehow cluttering up his life, and he'd become too embarrassed to ask her to leave?

But she didn't want to go!

She thought her heart might just slide down to her shoes as the knowledge thumped against it like a hammer.

Why, that was ludicrous! Why not? This opportunity was one she'd wanted for years. She wanted to do so much with her designs, work with exciting fabrics, achieve great looks and find new ways to use old ideas. She had *ambitions,* like many other young women in New York—aspirations to rise to the top of her field.

That didn't ease the ache in her heart. A dozen memories assailed her—of the fun she and Honor had created learning history, of their day on in-line skates, of the constant teasing, especially when Chad was home. It gave her a zest for his company. His kisses had given her a desire for more. Many more.

Maybe a lifetime full of them.

The class finished, and the instructor gave instructions for the students to attend additional rehearsals this week and next. Honor and Leilani signed up for the extra afternoon rehearsal.

Spring felt stifled, and restlessly walked around

the hall for the time it took one class to empty, as other dancers filed in. The girls moved into the rehearsal hall, and milled about.

She had to get out for a bit. Stroll the street and think, or she'd end up with a huge headache.

What she really wanted was to talk with Autumn. But she couldn't do that face to face, and besides, her sister had planned to be out today.

Lord, she prayed. *I need to talk to someone or burst.* Spring glanced at her watch. Her friend Dana would be at the church about now.

She spun on her heel and found Honor.

"Honor, you and Leilani are set here for the afternoon. You don't need me for this, and I need to run out for a little while. The two of you come home right after the rehearsal, all right? Straight home. No side trips."

"Okay. You'll be home when I get there?"

"I think so. I'm just going to run by the church on my way home to talk with Dana about, um, those other costumes I'm doing. I won't be too long."

On her way, the thoughts kept racing through her mind like a runaway subway train. She couldn't leave Honor now. So grown up in some ways, Honor still depended on her to be around at a mere call. If she went, the child would feel abandoned once again, as she and Autumn had.

Lord, I didn't realize I felt abandoned. Autumn and I...we always had each other. We had Uncle William.

Honor had Chad, though. Spring wasn't exactly abandoning the girl. Though Chad wasn't always available to his sister at every turn, if Spring went, Honor would still have him.

Spring envied that. Honor would always have Chad.

Suddenly she knew that swelling tidal wave of reluctance to leave New York centered more on Chad than it did on Honor. A pain sliced through her heart at the mere thought of putting that much distance between them. She felt like crying.

Did Chad know she loved him?

The knowledge of her love grew and mushroomed, filling her mind and heart until it crowded out everything else. She was unabashedly in love with Chad Alexander. Their kisses had fired a yearning for him beyond mere passion.

That attraction between them was very apparent. She couldn't ignore it, nor did she want to. He'd wanted her, too. More than once, more than just…physically. His gaze had been filled with tenderness when he'd held her close—a growing wonder of understanding when they'd shared their childhood experiences. That tenderness crept into hollows in her heart she hadn't known were there.

Lord, he does have feelings for me. I know it. Why doesn't he say it? Why doesn't he admit he loves me?

Or did he know, and refused to acknowledge it? Perhaps it wasn't enough. The awful thought seared her. Were they so wrong for each other? Was she the wrong kind of woman to make him a good life partner?

Arriving at the church, she hurried down the halls to the office. Thankfully, Spring found her friend at the copy machine, while other church staff darted about like ants in an anthill. Smiling, Dana told her she wasn't at all adverse to taking a break.

They chose to sit in a pew at the rear of the church auditorium, while Spring poured out her confusion and feelings. She finally said, "Dana, I don't know what to do. What to say. Am I nuts for wanting to say thanks-but-no-thanks to Paris? It just doesn't feel right to leave at this time. Honor and Chad need me. I—" She sighed, brushing her bangs aside. A headache edged against her temples. How could loving someone be so baffling?

"But?"

"But I can't go on living there, either, in that apartment, loving Chad the way I do. In spite of my concerns for Honor. I couldn't stand the heartbreak if he—" she shook her head, fighting the tears that threatened to slide down her cheeks "—if he doesn't really want me. But I can't think of why he'd arrange for me to leave if he does."

"Then you'll have to ask him outright, I guess," Dana replied briskly. "Women have more often than not taken the initiative in matters of the heart, if you ask me. We have many examples of women who lead rather than follow. But first, let's ask God's help, shall we?''

Together, the two women knelt at the pew. Dana prayed simply, asking for God's direction for Spring. Then Spring felt a welling faith enter her heart and soul, an assurance of God's love. It calmed her. Her own words came easily, surprising her with their pouring forth.

"Oh, Father, thank you for your love. I never knew before moving to New York how much I needed it. Thank you for showing me the way to love. For opening my heart to understanding what faith is, faith in You. In Jesus. Now lead me, Father, to clear my mind to see what I should do. I need your wisdom in this dilemma, to make the right choices. I'll accept—''

Her voice cracked. Could she pray to accept it if Chad didn't really love her?

But he did want her.

Mere wanting wasn't enough. But if he didn't want a marriage, could she let him go?

She swallowed hard. Not knowing if she had that kind of strength, she nevertheless finished her prayer with a whisper. *"If Chad doesn't love me...enough, I'll have to accept that.''*

The day had been hot and humid. Ignoring Chad's note for them to eat out, Spring made salads for supper. She mixed a huge pitcher of iced tea, and bought sherbet for dessert.

She smiled. For once, she and Chad were to enjoy an evening alone. Dana had impishly suggested they needed a real date—at least one evening to find out if they could be a couple—and she'd fix it so they could.

Dana called five minutes after Honor got home and asked that Honor and Leilani join the church's teen council; they were meeting tonight over pizza. Dana promised to see that both teens were escorted home by a responsible adult.

Honor had left in a cab ten minutes ago.

Spring put in a favorite CD to play, one with energy and a snappy beat. Even though the evening sun still warmed the apartment, she lit the candles on the dining room table.

She ran back to her room to change into her soft turquoise knit, then dashed back to the kitchen to place crusty rolls into a warming oven. Chad's key turned in the door. He called, "Honor?"

She should let him come all the way into the apartment before answering, Spring decided. Let the mood settle over him a moment.

"What's happening?" he said next. "Candles on the table? The good dinnerware? I thought we'd eat out. Where are you?"

"Oh, Honor's gone to a teen meeting at church." Spring let her voice drift from the kitchen. She waited for his answer, but none came. What was he thinking? What was he making of the intimate table setting?

She took a step around the kitchen door to see into the main room, just as the phone rang. Standing near the desk, his hand undoing his tie, he glanced at her.

"I thought you'd be out celebrating or packing or something."

"I'm not sure that will be necessary."

"You don't?" He frowned.

The phone continued to ring. "You arranged for my acceptance into LaSalle, didn't you."

"Is that a problem?" Pursing his mouth, he slid out of his jacket and placed it on the desk chair.

"It could be."

"Why? What do you mean?"

A second later, the answering machine clicked on. "Hey, Chad, this is Kevin. Need to ask a question, buddy. Old Jackson's breathing down my neck about a certain client—"

Chad snatched up the phone, his annoyance barely contained. "Hello."

His frown deepened. He continued to stare at her. She tipped her head at him, giving a tentative smile. A flirtatious smile, she hoped. If he didn't want her, this was his chance to change the way the evening would go.

His eyes darkened. With one hand, he pulled his already loosened tie from around his neck and tossed it over his shoulder. Spring watched it flutter to the floor.

She took another step toward him. His gaze

locked into hers. "Oh?" He kept speaking, though she thought—she hoped—he was quickly losing interest in the conversation. He held the phone away from his mouth, his indrawn breath sharp.

The current between them felt as though someone had just plugged in the whole city with new lights. It gave her the courage to say exactly what she wanted.

"I don't want to leave New York, Chad." She held her breath and waited. "I don't want to leave you."

His expression intensified, questions raging there. After a moment, he said into the phone, "Um, Kevin, I'll talk to you on—on Monday, all right? But I'm not available for the rest of the weekend. Understand?"

The receiver clanked on its base.

Only a heartbeat skipped by before his raspy invitation. "Okay. Now say that again. Please?"

Spring propelled herself forward, her heart beating in triple time.

And promptly tripped over the briefcase in her path.

Chapter Nineteen

"Oooph!" A pain-filled cry burst from Spring. Agony shot through her big toe and up her shin. She hopped, squeezing her eyes tightly closed against the excruciating agony. "Oh…oh…oh…"

She hit something hard with her hopping foot, then came down again solidly against her arch. She teetered.

The offending briefcase thumped as it fell flat.

Chad bit back an oath as he lunged toward her. He caught her, sliding his arms around her to gather her close. "Steady, sweetheart, I've got you now. You stumbled over that…silly briefcase."

"Oh…" she groaned. Her face against his shoulder, she dug her fingers into his arms and clung until the first wave of pain could pass.

"I'm so sorry," he said above her. Even through the numbing pain, the vibrations of his deepened voice sent waves of comfort into her body. "I shouldn't have left it in the middle of the floor. What hurts?"

"Toe," she mumbled.

"Can you walk?"

She shook her head. The pain still felt too new, too sharp.

He held her for a moment, gently rocking her from side to side. She barely breathed through the pounding pain, gritting her teeth to hold back the tears. Then ever so slowly, the pain lessened a degree.

His shirt collar flapped against her cheek. She turned her head, finding the base of his throat with the tip of her nose and the curve of her lips. He still smelled faintly of aftershave. She pulled a deep breath, loving the way his pulse pounded, the way it felt to be nestled in his arms.

The slightest of quivers rumbled through his chest. She felt them, like warnings of an earthquake.

Now it was he who groaned. He scooped her up, carrying her with long strides to the sofa. He lay her down, then snatched a pillow to put under her head. She scooted herself into a sitting position against the sofa arm.

"Still hurt?" he asked. He went to his knees beside the sofa.

"Mmm-hmm." She nodded, her lips pressed together.

He reached and turned on the table lamp, filling

shadows where the lowering sunlight couldn't reach. Glancing at her face, he brushed a thumb beneath her eye. He rubbed the moisture he'd found there between his fingers. Compassion filled his tone as he said, "I'm so sorry, sweetheart. Really sorry."

"It's my own fault," she muttered. "That'll teach me to go barefoot."

She tried to laugh, tried to make light of her injury, but the sound came out shaky.

"Aw, sweetheart." He brushed her hair from her eyes, then pressed a light gentle kiss against her mouth. He leaned to kiss her again, then stopped.

Abruptly, he yanked his gaze away and turned his attention to her foot. He ran a hand down her shin and cradled her foot in his long fingers.

"Oh, boy!" He sucked in his breath. Beneath his summer tan, his skin paled. "Spring, honey, I think we'd better let a doctor check this out."

"Oh, no. It's only a stubbed toe."

"Uh-huh. But it's already turning dark and it's swelling. I think you've broken it."

"But I've stubbed a toe before," she said in protest. Finally, she bent her knee, pulling her foot closer to her body for a peek. It did look awful. "And against a much harder surface, like a concrete step. It's always painful, but I've never broken it. After a few days, it heals."

"This time you've done it." He rose and reached for the desk phone. "I'll get a cab. I know where there's a twenty-four-hour clinic. We'll have faster service there than in a hospital emergency room.''

"Don't, Chad. There isn't much that can be done for a broken toe, anyway. I'll just rest here for a little while. It'll get better.''

"Not this time.''

Chad was adamant. While waiting for the cab, he called the church and sent a message to Honor, gathered Spring's purse and sandals for her, and carried her to the elevator.

"I can hobble,'' she insisted. Her bare feet dangled over his arm, and she tugged to make sure her skirt was as modestly draped as she could manage. She felt heat climb her cheeks as she thought how much leg she must be showing. Oh, why hadn't she changed into slacks?

She bit her lip against a sweeping wave of added embarrassment when the elevator doors opened to reveal two elderly women. One clutched a tiny poodle to her chest. After one glance at her and Chad, they slanted their eyes toward each other in a telling way, then stared straight ahead.

"Broken toe,'' Chad said by way of explanation.

One woman's mouth tightened, but otherwise she ignored them. The elevator's hum began as the doors closed. The poodle yipped and climbed to his owner's shoulder to stare at Spring.

"There, there, Lambkin,'' the woman murmured as she stroked her pet, then covered the poodle's eyes with her hand. She sniffed. "One must keep one's eyes to oneself."

Spring giggled in spite of her pain. "Only in New York," she whispered into Chad's ear.

Chad raised a brow, a responding smile tugging at the corners of his mouth. He lowered her to stand, propped in the corner. His hand remained firmly under her elbow while his head bent to hers.

"My darling! I can't stand it any longer. Will you run away to the moon with me?" he asked in a whisper just loud enough to fill the tiny enclosure.

"To the moon and back, my dearest," she responded in kind, putting a lilt in her voice. "We'll leave all this mundane world behind and fly away to live in bliss together."

The elevator doors opened. Lester stood nearby.

"Afternoon, Miss Goodley. Mrs. Smith. Hope your little Lambkin is well today."

The woman, who had remained silent until now, spoke while they made a beeline for the front door as though fearing a contagion in the air. "We won't linger to talk today if you don't mind, Lester," said Mrs. Smith.

"What's with them?" Lester asked.

"Just a little nonsense on our part, I'm afraid," Chad admitted, and grinned. He bent and lifted Spring once more. At least it had diverted her from the pain for a few moments, he silently noted. "Broken toe. Got that taxi handy?"

"Sure thing, Mr. Alexander. Sorry you're hurt, Miss Barbour."

"It's not a major wound, thank God," Spring responded. She placed the back of her hand on her forehead and dramatized. "I guess I'll live to serve another day."

They left the building to Lester's laughter.

Then a troubling question reared in her thoughts. Thank God, indeed, she'd live to serve another day. But where would that be? In Paris? In New York, on her own again? Or here…where she belonged?

She sighed, no longer feeling amused.

Hearing the sigh, Chad paused at the taxi door. His gaze delved into hers, invading all her senses with a great, sweet tenderness that went beyond anything she'd ever known. It melted all her insides. Spring wanted to stay where she was forever.

"We're going to continue that conversation, you know," he murmured as he placed her into the cab. His lips were very close to hers for a moment.

"Which one?"

"The one we'd started before all this craziness began. When you said you didn't want to leave. But first we're going to find help for your poor toe."

"Chad—"

"Nope. Not another word until we're back home."

"Home?"

"Yes, home. Together. And then we'll talk all night if that's what it takes. Agreed?"

Nearly three hours later, Spring placed her feet firmly on the sidewalk as she prepared to leave another taxi. She wore an oversize encasement shoe on her left foot, her sandal on her right. Chad paid the driver, then took her elbow. She'd never felt more exhausted in her life.

Upstairs, Honor was all over them as soon as they entered the apartment. "What happened? Does it hurt a lot? Are you going to have to stay off it for a while? You're not leaving, are you? Please tell me. I don't want you to leave—"

"Slow down, Honor. Let Spring sit."

"But Mrs. Feathers called," Honor continued, as Spring hobbled into the living room and perched on the edge of the big chair. "She wants you to return a call to talk about going to Paris. She said you've got a scholarship with a fancy design school there."

Honor's worried eyes stared at her with a child's woe. Her voice wavered. "You aren't going to accept it, are you, Spring?"

"I don't know yet, Honor." She was thankful the pain medication had kicked in. Only that promise of a long talk with Chad kept her from going straight to bed. "Not right away, at least."

"I thought you were happy with us," Honor said, her lips quivering.

"Honor, we don't own Spring," Chad said gently before she'd formed an answer. "She's a free agent, and we've been taking all her time and attention for ourselves for months. Don't you see it? Spring has no time for her own pursuits anymore because she's so busy taking care of us. She has to get her own life back. She has her own heart's desire to follow.''

So that was it? He was letting her go?

Honor's brown eyes filled with tears. "I'm sorry, Spring. Do you really want to go?''

Spring tried to catch Chad's gaze, but he wasn't looking at her. Or wouldn't. He pulled out the contents of his pockets and laid them on his desk.

"Don't distress yourself, honey,'' she answered through dry lips. How would she stand it if he really wanted her to leave, after all? "Nothing is set in stone, you know.''

"We'd be totally selfish to ask her to give up this chance,'' Chad said. At that moment, his dark lashes swept upward. She caught a flash of pure misery in those blue depths.

Her heart lifted. Was he simply playing noble for her sake? Though tired, she pushed herself to sit more comfortably.

"Do you want a cup of tea?'' Honor asked. "Should I help you to bed?''

"Thanks, sweetie, but I'm fine. Honest. And my activities may be curtailed a bit with clumsiness for a week or two, but I can still take care of myself. There's nothing to worry about.''

"Sure?''

"Yes, I'm sure.''

"Go on to bed now, Honor,'' Chad said. "I want to talk with Spring a while.''

"But—"

"I'm sure Spring won't make any decisions without you being the first to know about them."

"Okay, I guess," Honor grumbled. She grimaced as she dragged herself off to bed. Her parting glare indicated she'd caught the fact she wasn't to have a part in making that decision.

"She's not a happy camper," he muttered. He ran a hand over the back of his neck.

"Not at the moment," Spring agreed, watching him.

He'd promised they would finish their discussion, but had their interruption given him too much time to think? Too many reasons why she should go?

He came toward her slowly. "Spring…"

"Hmm?"

"Did you mean it?"

Her heart gave a sudden thump. There wasn't a coy bone in her body; she didn't pretend not to know what he meant. Slowly, she nodded. She wanted to stay with every fiber of her being—if she could stay as his wife. If he loved her as she loved him.

Yet, need wasn't the same as love.

And if he didn't love her?

All her emotions balled together in her middle. It hurt, clamping her heart and mind into knots.

Lord, if this isn't Your plan for my life, then help us deal with this desire we feel for each other. I don't know how to say no to Chad. I know he wants me on one level…physically…but he needs me on

many others, too. But will his need and my love be
enough on which to build a lifetime together? Lord,
please help me to see...to hear...to know.

As he had earlier that evening, Chad knelt before
her. He sat back on his heels, his hands on his thighs.
For a moment, he simply searched her face, probing
all her secrets and feelings. "Did you mean what
you said?"

"Yes," she whispered.

"You'd give up this chance—an incredible opportunity to study with the LaSalle School of Design—to stay with Honor and me?"

"Yes."

"Why?"

How could she say it? With all she'd read in his
eyes, he hadn't yet spoken of his own feelings.

She took a deep breath. "You need me here."

"Uh-huh. That's more than true. I'd be—I will
be—floundering in my own incompetence on the
home front, if you're not here. But that's no reason
to stay."

"I think it's a very strong reason, but..."

"But what?"

She bit her lip. "I have to ask you a barefaced
question, and I want you to be absolutely honest and
straightforward in your answer."

She took another deep breath, then caught her bottom lip between her teeth. She had to find the courage somewhere, she mused.

Then he startled her by taking her hand and speaking first. "Do you love me?"

"How did you know that was my question?"

His thumb caressed her palm, stroking in circles. It sent shivers up her spine.

"Because it is mine. Now answer me, barefaced and straightforward." His gaze fixed on her mouth, seeming to watch her lips as she formed her words. His voice dipping to a near whisper, he asked again, "Do you love me?"

Didn't he *know?* She wanted to laugh and shout her love from the roof of their building. From the Empire State building. From the World Trade Center. Taking out billboards to announce Spring Loves Chad wouldn't be enough...if he wanted her for the right reasons.

"Yes," she whispered. Her voice shook, her hands trembled. She tried to keep her answer light, tried to give him a way out if he couldn't accept it. "The Lord knows—and so does everyone else, I expect—that I do. Haven't I made a sufficient fool of myself by wearing my heart on my sleeve? You don't have to do anything about it if you don't...choose to."

Tightening his hold on her hand, he bowed his head over it. She pushed her fingers through his rich dark brown hair with her other hand. She loved the soft way it felt as she fingered it. She even gained the courage to run her thumb across his brow, noting the texture of his skin, of his eyebrow.

"Now it's your turn."

"Yes."

"Yes?"

"Yes, I love you. There's never been anyone who's touched my heart the way you have. With you, I'm content with home. You make me want to gather all my primitive forces and build a stronghold to protect you and the babies we might have. You and Honor complete my life."

He raised his head, and she saw the pain in his eyes, deepening the blue to midnight. "I love you enough to let you go. You're so young still—you haven't even hit your mid-twenties. How can I take all your youth and risk your waking up one day to regrets?" He shook his head. "I want you to develop your talent. I want to let you do what your heart tells you."

"What if my heart tells me that my life is here? With you and Honor?"

"You say that now—"

"Chad, it isn't impossible. Really, it isn't. Don't you see? Honor won't need either of us much longer. She'll be off to college in only a few years, and then we'll be on our own. I'll have years ahead to go after my ambitions."

"Time of our own…that sounds like a wonder." He laughed shakily. "I love my sister, but I'd give my right arm to have a year-long honeymoon with only you, squirreled away in a small hotel someplace in Europe."

His confession sent shivers through her. Feeling it, his back straightened. He tentatively kissed her, then made a sound deep in his throat and drew her even closer.

Finally, he pulled away. He leaned his forehead gently against hers. "You see how it is. I'd be so jealous of anywhere else you'd spend your time."

"Not any more than I already am," she whispered.

Which called for another brush of his lips. "But what if we have kids of our own?" he asked between kisses.

"I'd like that. Would you?"

"Uh-huh. Several. But that would really tie you down. What of your ambitions then?"

"Chad, I've discovered something about myself lately. I do love design, fashion or otherwise. But it doesn't have to be haute couture to make me happy."

"Are you sure?"

"I've already thought about it, Chad. I'm having just as much fun and satisfaction doing those Noah's Ark costumes for the church. And you recall that woman I met while waiting for Honor's ballet class to finish? I've talked to her again. I think we can work together. We're going to meet next week to show each other our work. There's lot of employment for a part-time designer in this city. And we'd do most of our work in her workroom." She grinned. "No more pins on the floor."

"As long as you keep them out of our room," Chad teased.

"Hooray!" The squeal came from the hallway.

Chad didn't even look his sister's way. He simply chuckled, his humor communicating a world of love with the woman he wanted to love all his life. "What are you doing up, child?"

"I had to make sure you did this right, didn't I? You haven't asked Spring to marry you yet."

"I'm about to do that right this minute. Will you, sweetheart?" He took a deep breath, then continued, "Will you be my wife?"

"In a New York heartbeat," she answered.

Two minutes later, through the misty world of their kisses, they heard Honor's voice. "Leilani? Guess what? It's happened...."

Spring was lost to all but Chad's wonderfully tender gaze.

* * * * *

Dear Reader,

God's word—Scripture—is as true today as yesterday, or two thousand years ago and longer. All of it is about relationships: relationships between God and mankind; between mankind and mankind; between husband and wife; parent and child; neighbor and neighbor. It covers all aspects of life. God teaches us that our answers to life's problems can be found in love.

I hope you like Spring and Chad's love story. Their struggles to balance their lives while "wanting it all" are as real as mine and yours, my daughter's and yours. Like Spring and Chad, I believe love *is* the key.

Ruth Scofield